0

Chapter 1

Kathy slumped in her SUV, at least as far as her tummy would allow, and peeked out the side of the door frame. The grass was getting high in the cemetery and she could barely see the plaque on the ground with her father's name etched on it. As she looked at the simple marker, small and insignificant amongst the many looming stones, she began to feel sadness rush in and settle upon her chest, wrapping it's burning hot fingers around her throat. Hopefully, the size of the marker didn't represent the size of the man or how loved or meaningful he was. The tiny little marker said nothing about the tragedy of her dad's life or death. It said nothing about the artistic genius who continually snuffed out his own light with insecurity and self-loathing. It said nothing about his ability to be an amazing dad full of pride and joy that ruined almost every moment by showing up drunk. He carried so much potential within himself and,

2

unfortunately, he would drown out the light forever for the sake of having just one more beer.

Kathy thought to herself about how much he would have hated his stupid little marker lying on top of his mother's own gravesite. He didn't ask to be buried with his mother. He didn't even want to be buried in their little hometown of Titusville, PA. He never felt he belonged there. As a matter of fact, he never felt he belonged anywhere. It would be a feeling he would pass down to Kathy over time. "Thank you very much for that, Dad," Kathy thought to herself. That stupid little marker on top of his mother's gravesite was all Kathy could do. When her brother showed up at her door and told her to sit down, that would be the beginning of the end of life as she knew it. Her brother, Will, told Kathy her father was found dead in his apartment where he must have laid for a couple days. How is that possible, one might wonder. He was lost in one of his drunken hazes where he always entered a world of darkness, leaving his daily life behind. He spent years coming and going out of everyday life so that when he was dead and gone, no one even noticed. When she found out he was dead, Kathy went through the motions that one must go through, including trying to figure out how on earth she would bury her father since that unexpected responsibility sat heavily upon her shoulders. He had no will or estate. He had no money in the bank. As far as she knew, he didn't really have anything to his name except for a few random pieces of artwork. When she went to meet with the funeral director, he handed her a tiny green envelope that had the words "personal effects" printed on the front of it. She slowly unzipped the little bag, hoping there would be something there to help her. Some answers or directions. Maybe even something telling her he had been thinking of her and that everything would be okay. But all she pulled out was a powder blue colored lighter with a naked, blonde woman printed on it, a set of keys, a crumpled up one-dollar bill, and seventy-three cents in change. That was it. On his dying day, his daughter would still have to find a way to take care of him. So, Kathy withdrew the remainder of her college tuition money and asked the funeral director what she could afford. That is how he ended up in ashes, on his mother's grave, with his stupid little marker.

She felt paralyzed while she was sitting in her car and her voice, dripping with pain, whispered," I don't know what to say to you, Dad." She knew what she had to say. There was something that she had been holding onto for a very long time now. Something she never told anyone. But she just couldn't talk to him. How could she talk to her father, now that he was dead, when she had gone months not talking to him when he was alive? With a broken heart and head full of guilt and shame, she urged herself to get out of the car and try to say something to him. But she was frozen, and no words would come to her. She was aware of the fact that she was doing the same thing she confronted her clients about when they tried to motivate themselves through "shoulds". She was "shoulding" on herself, trying to guilt herself to get out of the car. She realized how much of her own internal dialogue included "shoulds" and, if she wasn't going to let her clients do that to themselves, maybe she shouldn't do it to herself either. On that note, she inhaled a slow, deep breath and then exhaled, loosening the grip of those fingers around her throat and lifting the weight off her chest. She sat up straight, shifted her weight beneath the steering wheel, and with head up high and eyes forward, she muttered the words, "another day", giving herself permission to wait until she was ready, then she drove the hell out of there.

The gravel crunched and protested under Kathy's tires and the sun flickered like a strobe light as it filtered through the trees lining the cemetery. As she reached the rusty, iron fence of the exit, she rolled her window down, inviting the freedom that lie in front of her. The sun now steady and warm upon her face and the intoxicating smell of autumn at her nostrils reminded her of all the beauty and joy that, if sought, could make life's difficulties more tolerable.

As Kathy drove down the street toward the center of town, she noticed how the golden yellow leaves hung from the maple trees lining the street, draping the sides and top of her view. Blue skies rested upon the distant pines and green fields lining the road to town and created a picture-perfect image. But things aren't always as they appear.

As Kathy's golden red curls blew in the breeze of her open car window, she thought of the busy day she had before her. She needed to go home and pick up Max and then take him over to her mother, Sarah's house. Sarah loved her "grand puppy", Max and looked forward to babysitting him when Kathy had a long day scheduled at work. After dropping off Max, Kathy would go to her office in the old town square building that rested on the corner of the city park.

She enjoyed the location in the summer when Titusville was all abuzz with the Oil Heritage Festival. The park was full of crafters and artists selling their goods. Kathy had many memories of her and her father participating in that and many other festivals and arts and crafts shows. They were both exciting and a huge pain in the ass. There was the hope of making some money to pay bills and buy food, and there was the reality of standing for hours, pretending to be something they weren't, turned "on" with proud smiles pasted on insecure faces, dealing with rain and wind and raging sunburns on fair, freckled skin. But, money or no money, Kathy's dad always made a feast for the day. He'd have a cooler filled with sodas and homemade egg and olive salad sandwiches. He'd bring potato chips, fruit-filled cookies, chocolate, and whatever other goodies he could find. All the treats helped to candy coat the reality that, with the admiration and praise he would receive that day, the title of town drunk awaited him for the next. As the daughter of the town drunk,

Kathy found that many of her memories, that would otherwise be pleasant, were experienced more as a twisted fond mortification.

Kathy pulled in her driveway and before she even exited her SUV, Max was standing in the window, his bark booming and beckoning for her to come in. She unlocked the door and steadied herself, preparing for Max to attack her with hugs and kisses when she came in. As big as Kathy was, he still had the power to knock her off balance. After lots of excited and slobber-filled kisses, she changed her clothes for work, trying not to let the boring, shapeless, and dark colored fat clothes bring her down. She leashed up Max, grabbed her briefcase and headed to Sarah's apartment.

After Max was all buckled in the back, Kathy started the car and headed to the small apartment where Sarah lived. "Are you going to be a good boy for Gramma today, Max?" Many pants and wines and tapping on Kathy's shoulder with his big golden-red paws followed. She pulled up to Sarah's apartment door and Max lunged out of the car, prancing and smiling wide to greet his grandma at the door. A "good boy" biscuit was graciously accepted and then he plopped heavily in the recliner where he would remain the rest of the day being pampered and spoiled.

"It's a little early for Christmas decorating, isn't it Mom?", Kathy asked when she noticed a box full of ornaments sitting beside the recliner.

"Yes, unfortunately so, but these are your brother's ornaments that I've been keeping for him. I thought I might take them over to him sometime soon. He hasn't responded to any of my texts or calls. I guess he is ignoring me again. He hasn't said anything to you about me, has he?"

"Mom! No, he hasn't said anything to me or even responded to any of my messages. I'm starting to worry about him. I think I might try to go see him this week. I'm not sure it's a good idea that you try to give him his ornaments, Mom. You know how he gets."

She just couldn't talk to Sarah today about the family drama, especially after trying to make some peace with her father earlier at the cemetery turned out to be an epic fail. Kathy felt like she was failing a lot these days, especially after her biggest failure of yet.... letting her dad die.

Chapter 2

It didn't take Kathy long to say goodbye to Sarah and Max and head to the office. She felt overwhelmed and disillusioned and still had a whole day of clients in front of her. Since she didn't stay long at her Mom's, Kathy had plenty of time after turning on all the lights and making coffee before her first client came in. She stocked bottles of water in the little refrigerator setting on the buffet by the coffee pot and turned the light on the fish tank where all her little guppies and goldfish were begging for food, especially Big Bessie. Kathy loved the soothing sound of the water bubbling softly through the fish tank filter. As a matter of fact, she loved her lobby altogether. From the four big, blue, comfortable chairs sitting around a coffee table and little end tables with large, white gourd shaped lamps and two floor lamps with oversized drum shades bent over two of the chairs. The walls were covered in black and white photographs of beaches and trees and all things relaxing. A big framed poster on one wall, the same color of the four chairs, had the word "breathe" in white, scrawled across it. She then went down the hall to the office where she met with her clients. That room was dimly lit with big round lamps that sat between four very large brown chairs. A small fountain sat on one of the end tables gently and softly pouring water down upon tiny stones which was lovely on most days, except when someone needed to use the bathroom. Large watery paintings hung on the walls. The other end stands contained boxes of Kleenex, bowls of candy and an overused, somewhat stretched out slinky. She plopped on her big, brown, cushy chair and tried to meditate for a few minutes before her long day started. She closed her eyes and took deep breaths and the thoughts just came pouring out. Like pushing the right button on a computer, every damn negative thing that happened to her and her family came rushing to the surface. She could have chosen to disengage but allowed herself to feel the pain and frustration.

Kathy knew Sarah taking Will his ornaments would not go well. It was always the same cycle with them, anymore. Resentment, rejection, broken heartedness and guilt. It just kept playing out over and over. The whole thing was getting old and Kathy was sick of it. All she ever wanted was to keep her family together and close but those two were just not cooperating with her. Her whole family has never cooperated with her.

There was trouble for Kathy's small family form the beginning when Kathy's mom, Sarah, fell in love with Will's father, Tom. Sarah came from a poor family of 16 brothers and sisters. When she met Tom, she didn't have any confidence in herself and fell fast for the tall and lanky young boy who made her feel special. She soon became pregnant, dropped out of school and gave birth to a baby boy, Will.

Even before Sarah gave birth, the boy who made her feel special, left her and walked out of her and their son's life, abandoning them both.

She was devastated but adored her baby boy. She met George when Will was just a toddler. George was a good-looking artist who always wore a sports jacket and jeans. He reminded Sarah of Kenny Rogers with his full, slightly graying hair and beard.

On the day of their wedding, Sarah, in her best blue dress, had to drag an intoxicated George out of the bar to marry her. She was determined to provide her son with a father, so she didn't even notice the red flags waving forewarnings.

Shortly after their marriage, Sarah gave birth to a baby girl named Kathy. Kathy became the apple of George's eye. Through the following years, George failed to treat Kathy and Will the same. This broke Sarah's heart for her young boy that she adored so deeply. She would begin to feel a need to overcompensate for what she ultimately failed to provide for her son. A father who showed him he loved him as much as she did.

For several years, Sarah, George, Will and Kathy would be a family and there would be some good times, but they were often overshadowed by George's drinking and their constant fighting. Sarah would become resentful toward George for his inability or unwillingness, whatever it may be, to provide for or meet her and her children's needs. She would work all day, just to walk all the way home and find him drunk on the couch with a car sitting out on the curb, having accomplished nothing that day.

Eventually, as the kids got older, and after a violent fight that involved George throwing the goulash Sarah had prepared, having spent the last of the food stamps, across the room and ripping the phone off the wall and slicing her hand open as she tried to call for help, she kicked him out. That was the last meal she would ever scrub off the wall. No more spaghetti noodles stuck on plaster or greasy fried chicken soaking through wallpaper. Kathy and Will witnessed too many of their meals hitting the walls rather than their bellies. Clearly food was love and hate to George. He was either gorging his family full of delicious and copious amounts of food or using it as a weapon, throwing it away as if it had no meaning or purpose at all.

Shortly after Sarah and George separated, Will's biological father, Tom, returned. He was a caller for a traveling carnival and played that gig for many years. When he arrived at Sarah's home, he embraced Will's cousin, mistaking him for Will. There would begin Tom's invalidation of Will and Will's ever-growing belief that he wasn't lovable or acceptable enough.

There was one more figure in Will's life who would reinforce that belief. It was his Uncle Bruce, Tom's brother. Bruce was the worst of all because he knew how to love, and he knew how to withdraw, reject, and abandon even better. He would invite Will into his life with the promise of acceptance and love celebrated over football games and homemade meals including juicy steaks and potatoes and then, two days later, refuse to let him in the building, avoid his phone calls, and tell him he didn't want his damn Christmas presents Will purchased special for him. His behavior was erratic and bipolar. He would prove to be unstable, unreliable and dangerous to anyone who needed to be loved and accepted by him, especially Will.

And last, all those years Sarah tried so hard to protect her son and let him know he was loved was lost when she decided to follow Will's father, Tom out on the carnival to be the next duck pond caller. That is the decision she would pay for the rest of her life. She left Will with her sister and Kathy with her alcoholic father, George. Will and Kathy became distanced by geography and that would be the beginning of Kathy's decent into an isolated and chaotic life with her drunken father.

A couple years would follow that consisted of Kathy going off to school in the morning, never knowing what to expect from her father, when the bus brought her home. She always dreaded when the bus rolled to a stop because he would either not be there to pick her up, so she would walk home alone, let herself in the apartment where there was no television or anything that a young girl could entertain herself with. She would curl up in a large chair by the window and wait for hours for her father to finally make it home reeking of stale beer and cigarettes. The other option was even worse. If her father was at the stop when the bus pulled in he would be drunk and either setting on the side walk or crawling behind her on his hands and knees, begging her to forgive him because she was upset and embarrassed that he was drunk. It was also not uncommon for George to be frustrated and angry at someone or something and randomly tear the artwork he was carrying to shreds and throwing them all over the streets. Either way she lived a childhood of being mortified and ashamed. Her classmates would stare and feel pity for her or laugh and giggle at her out of control father.

Whether she was waiting in the chair for hours or being embarrassed out on the streets, she ate. She stuffed herself. If there

17

was food, she devoured it. She was empty and desperately wanted to be filled up. And, filled up, she became.

Sarah and Tom would finally establish residency in another state where her children would reunite with their mother. Ultimately, they would return to Titusville until Kathy and Will graduated high school.

The day Kathy went to college, Sarah and Tom left the state again. Kathy spent her first year of college feeling abandoned and insecure. She was in a new environment away from home and shared a room with a popular girl who came to school with an already well-established group of friends. Kathy didn't feel she fit into the group and, at first, felt alone. Who would give her advice and support when she needed it? Who would send her care packages of homemade cookies, new underwear, and a 100-count box of new pens, obviously, because you can never have enough? Her dad tried. This was a time when he was managing to be sober so on weekends he would drive to college, take Kathy out to lunch, and then take her grocery shopping for a week's worth of macaroni and cheese and little cans of beanie wienies.

After a failed attempt to relocate, Sarah and Tom returned to Titusville one last time. And that is where they finally decided to stay. In time, Will would repay Tom's chronic invalidating when Tom, laying on his deathbed years later, calling for his son, died alone, never having seen the son he consistently rejected again.

Through all the comings and goings of Sarah and Tom, Kathy and Will developed feelings toward Sarah would be expressed in different ways. Will became full of rage and hateful, pushing his mother away. Kathy stuffed her feelings deep inside and became overly protective and desperate to make both her brother and mother get along. Unfortunately, she never acknowledged her own anger until many years and layers of fat later. The anger Kathy had suppressed regarding her mother exploded one day after the two women had a small disagreement. Sarah had never seen her daughter act so livid and out of control. Kathy would find her mouth screaming words she would have never consciously chosen to say to her mother, but they simply erupted out of the darkness and oozed over her mother, burning her along the way. Sarah would end up never fully understanding the origin of Kathy's reaction and just how deep that molten, raw pain and anger ran. It crept beneath her skin for years carving out pieces of Kathy, creating a geography, she didn't even recognize. It left, in its path, a foreign land full of dirt and debris, but, lying below, existed many treasures. Treasures that she was slowly beginning to excavate.

Kathy was so wrapped up in her distant thoughts and memories about her family that she was startled by the sound of the outside door leading into the lobby of her office. Her client, Janice, must have arrived.

Chapter 3

Janice started seeing Kathy for therapy about six months ago,
although the two women knew each other for many years. Janice's
husband, Brad, was the manager of Kathy's office building when she
was just starting out in private practice. When he first took over
managing his uncle's rental business, Brad's wife, Janice used to pop
in from time to time to collect the monthly rent payments if he was
busy in another area of town. Kathy found Janice to be kind and
somewhat soft-spoken. They would chit chat a little about the day
but never too in depth. Once, Janice had shared with Kathy that she
was separated from her family in Florida and missed them terribly.
But, she then became guarded and stated she had to get home. Kathy
had invited her a couple of times to stay for a short while and talk or
have coffee, but Janice never accepted the invite. Kathy got the
sense that Janice didn't get out of the house often. She wondered if it
was because she was a young mother with a baby in tow or if there

may be something else going on. Kathy didn't care much for Brad. Whenever he would come around Kathy's office, she felt her hair stand up on the back of her neck. She couldn't help but think he had something to do with Janice's odd behavior. Eventually, Janice quit coming in altogether. After not seeing her for several months, Kathy called to speak with Janice, but she was short and distant with her. Kathy began to be concerned for the young woman and told her, if she ever needed to talk to anyone, Kathy would be there for her. Kathy would not hear from Janice for years and, eventually, she moved into a new office space to accommodate her growing practice. It was a very pleasant surprise when Kathy received a call from Janice a few months ago. She was ready to talk but it was imperative that it be kept secret.

Janice stated her husband could not find out she was seeking counseling, so she couldn't use her health insurance. Kathy offered to meet with her and discuss what was going on at home and discuss payment options. It didn't take Kathy long to see that Janice was in a dire situation and had no personal income to rely on. She believed the woman was unsafe and alone and there was no way Kathy would ever turn her back on her, so she offered to see Janice pro bono for a few visits. During Janice's intake evaluation, she shared with Kathy that there was domestic violence occurring at home, validating Kathy's initial suspicions years ago. Janice hadn't shared this with anyone and was afraid to say it out loud but, she knew, if she was going to get help, and, most importantly, protect her daughter, she had to be completely honest. The fear of being judged kept her from owning her truth for too long but, now things were escalating, and she was worried about her daughter. Now that she felt her daughter may be affected by what was happening at home, she couldn't deny the problems one minute longer.

Janice and Kathy agreed that their treatment plan would consist of domestic violence education, coping and self-esteem. Over the last six months Janice disclosed more about her husband's history of violent behavior and the overall unhealthy characteristics of the relationship. The two women discussed characteristics of abuse and cycles of violence. Kathy was becoming more concerned about Janice as it seemed she was describing tension building in the relationship. Kathy warned Janice that she needed to be safe in case the violence escalated. She provided Janice with a card for the local domestic violence shelter and spent the day's session going over safety planning with her.

By the end of the session, Janice had a few steps to consider in establishing a safety plan including having a packed bag in a secret place that she could quickly grab, asking a neighbor to call the police if he or she saw the porch light that stayed on all day and night turned off or having a friend or family member on speed dial so that if they were to receive a call from her and she was not on the other line, they were to call the police and send them to Janice's house. She may never have to use any of those safety steps, but it was important to have one or two of them in place. Her homework assignment was to consider the options and decide which ones she would like to implement.

After Janice, there were a string of other folks in and out of Kathy's office. Courageous men and women shared their stories of pain and fear, resentment and discouragement, guilt and self-doubt, and grief and loneliness. Each one trying to find their way through the darkness, to set themselves free from the burdens they carry and to heal their brokenness. They all wanted to be better, to be worthy, and to be lovable. And then there was Sam. Kathy had an especially disturbing session with Sam. He was a remarkable artist, full of potential, who was also bipolar. He was a walking dichotomy between being animated and full of energy and light to being deep in oppressive darkness. Unfortunately, Sam also abused alcohol and participated in the use of heroin. Kathy had referred him to several addictions programs and specialists since he started counseling a couple of months before. His last question to Kathy during his session left her feeling hopeless in her ability to help him.

"What if I don't want to stop using?" he asked.

"Then you will be in serious risk of losing your life someday, Sam."

"So be it, then", he said, shrugging his shoulders and smiling at her as he walked out of her office.

Why didn't he want to get better like the others? She felt so frustrated and afraid for him. All she wanted to do was save him. He didn't seem to want to be saved. He didn't seem to want anything from her but someone to talk to.

She was left feeling hopeless and helpless. That damn feeling of panic slipped itself around her throat again and she felt herself having an intense reaction to his lack of concern for his own life or desire to be saved. The question was, why was she being so strongly affected by Sam.

The long day and her session with Sam had her depleted. Her stomach hurt, her head pounded, and she just wanted to go home. Just as she sat down in her chair with a cool bottle of water, she heard the office door open again. She had one more session left and that was a new couple coming in for a consultation. She took a few deep breaths and grabbed a clipboard containing paperwork.

When Kathy opened the door to the lobby, she seen a man and a woman seated separately. The man sat on one side of the coffee table and the woman sat on the other side, opposite to him. Both had their heads down and were on their cell phones. Kathy never realized how big her lobby was until she saw the distance between these two souls.

"Excuse me. Are you Andrew and Linda? The Scutellas?" They both looked up and greeted Kathy. She explained that she needed to have them complete some paperwork before they began so Linda got up and came over toward Andrew and Kathy. Kathy kneeled beside Andrew to go over the documents when she looked up, her eyes met his and they were the sweetest and warmest eyes she had ever seen. He was tall and solid with long dark curls. His wife was also tall but was thin and lovely with bright blue eyes and luxurious, curly blonde hair. Kathy lifted her weight painfully from her kneeling position and left them to finish reading and signing the material.

Kathy led the couple back to her office where they went back to setting separately from one another. They were turned away from each other and had arms and legs crossed. Kathy moved her chair a bit to sit in the middle and across from them. She then started the session by asking them what made them decide to come in for counseling. Dr. and Mrs. Scutella both discussed their dissatisfaction regarding their marriage. They both felt unhappy and unfulfilled. They stated they had both considered leaving the marriage after participating in counseling a while ago. They stated it hadn't really helped and the distance was continuing to grow between them. This would be the last attempt at counseling. They planned on either repairing the relationship or having help terminating it forever.

Kathy asked the Scutellas what they would need to see to continue working on the relationship. They both shared they didn't feel loved or cared for and that they needed to start feeling more appreciated.

Kathy talked to them about love languages. She told them that partners demonstrate and experience love in different ways. This seemed to interest the couple and each partner expressed a desire to gain insight into what their love languages might be. Kathy provided the couple with individual questionnaires and explained that the love languages were physical touch, words of affirmation, quality time, acts of service and gift giving. Kathy concluded the session by asking them to complete the questionnaires, so they could discuss their results during their next meeting.

After walking the Scutellas out, Kathy finished up her work and then closed the office. She would pick Max up at Sarah's tomorrow morning which was the start of her long weekend. She was exhausted and starving so she picked up drive through and continued her way home with the window down. It was cold, but she needed the air. She found herself driving by homes with windows lit up in the darkness and wondered what everyone else was doing that evening. Were all the people in the homes surrounded by loved ones? Were they playing games or watching tv? Were there couples holding each other on the sofa or dancing in the middle of the living room floor? Or were there people, sitting all alone in the ear-piercing silence like she would soon be?

Kathy finally made it home and opened her front door, letting herself into the darkness. She clicked on the tv, took her food out of its greasy, brown bag and stuffed her feelings of emptiness.

Chapter 4

Kathy got up early the next day. She still felt tired and sluggish, not sure if it was from the extra-long day or the fact that she stuffed herself full of greasy food right before going to bed. She had to get rolling, though, since she and Sarah had plans to grab lunch and go to the movies together. Kathy hadn't seen a movie in the theater for a couple of years and was looking forward to seeing the new science fiction movie just released.

After lunch, Kathy and Sarah headed to the movie theater and stood in line for what seemed like hours. They finally purchased their tickets and found their way to the concession stand for sodas.

By the time they arrived at the right theater is was almost completely packed. Seats were limited, and Kathy began feeling panic coursing through her body as she worried if there would be enough room for her. She became hypersensitive to others' reactions as she and her mother walked up and down the aisle, trying to find a reasonable open area of seats. Her ears tuned into snickers and comments like, "Oh, great!" as she headed toward any row. The girls finally found a spot that looked good enough for the two of them to get to. As Kathy tried to squeeze in and step over people to get into the middle of the row where the seats were, she could hear a group of teenagers making pig and cow sounds. She knew they were intended for her, but she kept a smile on her face and humbly thanked the folks in the aisle for allowing her through. Her cheeks were crimson, and she felt embarrassed but continued to persist. Sarah sat down in the first seat and Kathy squeezed herself into the chair next to her. She wasn't sure what hurt more; her ass being squeezed in the seat, her ego, or her heart.

What was supposed to be a fun beginning to the weekend was taking a less than desirable turn. She didn't want to ruin her mom's good time, so she just pretended all was well. By time the movie was over, Kathy vowed she would never return their again unless, somehow, some way, she could finally figure out how to remove herself from the burden of her weight. She didn't have a problem with being fat. She had a problem with being in pain and limited by her body.

Kathy drove Sarah home and visited for a while and then leashed up Max and headed home to nurse her wounds and lay low for the rest of the weekend.

After some nursing, Kathy decided she would try to start taking some steps toward getting her body healthier and cooperating with her a little more. She was torn between loving herself as she was and appreciating her curves and trying to lose some weight, but what she did know for sure, was it was hard for her to try to love her body when it was hurting her and preventing her from living the full life she wanted for herself. It was also hard to be a therapist who was there to help her clients achieve their goals when she struggled with her own. She secretly felt like a hypocrite, but she was human too. She decided she would be patient with herself and just try to make choices that would contribute to her starting to feel better in her body.

Chapter 5

Before Kathy knew it, the weekend had come and gone, and it was time to head back to work. She knew her first client of the day was Janice and Kathy was getting more and more concerned about her.

Janice shared with Kathy when she came in for her appointment, "Things have been really intense at home lately so I'm going to try to lighten things up by taking Emily out tonight to get our Halloween pumpkin." Earlier that morning, Janice added up all the spare change she had been saving and was thrilled to see she had gathered eight dollars and fifty-seven cents. After meeting with Kathy and picking Emily up at school, she and her daughter walked to the market house on the corner of their neighborhood. Janice found the pumpkins they could afford with the money she saved and then told Emily she could choose which ever one she wanted. Emily seemed apprehensive about selecting her favorite.

"What if dad gets mad?" Emily asked.

"Honey, why would Daddy be mad?"

"Because when I asked him last week if we could get one he said it was a waste of money and a pumpkin would just rot anyway."

"It's okay, Sweetie, I'm sure he was just having a bad day. He will love our pumpkin," Janice comforted her little girl, heart-broken that her sweet daughter, only eight years old, had to carry those types of concerns.

When Janice and Emily got home, Janice put dinner in the oven and then lined the table with newspaper. She pulled out the pumpkin carving kit, turned on the radio, and the girls began carving their masterpiece. They sang and giggled and threw pumpkin goo at one another. After the pumpkin was all carved and displayed proudly in the middle of the table, Janice asked Emily, "So what should we name him?"

Emily stated, "Let's call him Jack. I can't wait until Daddy sees him. Isn't he so cute Mommy?"

She smiled at her sweet little girl and brushed her bangs out of her eyes, "Yes, Sweetie, He's adorable. Just like you."

And then Janice noticed it was getting late. Brad would be home soon, and they needed to get the pumpkin mess cleaned up before he got home. Just then, Brad opened the door.

"Oh, hi, Honey. How was your day?" Janice asked.

"It was a day. I'm starving. What's for dinner?"

When he entered the kitchen, and seen the pumpkin seeds still on the paper Brad furrowed his brows and, with disgust, snarled, "What the fuck is going on?"

Before Janice could open her mouth, Emily wrapped her little arms around Brad's leg and said, "Hi Daddy. Look what Mommy and I did today. This is Jack."

"I thought I told you that you didn't need a stupid pumpkin. And just how did you get the money to pay for the damn thing, Janice?"

"Emily, why don't you go wash your hands and get ready for dinner?" she told her daughter as she turned to Brad and quietly explained, " It was my spare change I saved over the last few months. Please don't ruin the fun for her, Brad." She was usually aware of his triggers, but she couldn't believe he was reacting like this in front of Emily over a Halloween pumpkin. Janice realized his fuse was becoming shorter and shorter lately and the tension was building fast. She sensed that the clouds were moving in and a big storm was forming.

"Bullshit. I know you took that money from me. Just who do you think you are spending my money on stupid shit she doesn't need? I work hard for that money. What the hell do you do? All you do is set in this house on your fat ass not doing a damn thing and then I have to come home to a mess. You can't even have dinner ready when I come home. Where the hell is dinner?'

"It's in the oven. Everything is done. I was just getting ready to get it out when you came in."

"Clean that shit off the table. I'll get the damn food out of the oven? You're about useless, Janice. What kind of slop did you make today anyway?"

Janice folded all the pumpkin seeds and innards into the paper and lifted Jack to wipe the table. Emily softly and slowly came down the stairs and entered the kitchen for dinner. Just as she sat down at her side of the table, Brad carried the heavy Dutch oven over to the table and dropped it carelessly onto the surface. As the heavy pot landed on the table, the lid popped off, splashing steaming hot, homemade bean soup and hitting Jack hard enough that he fell over and rolled off the table, breaking into several pieces.

"Oh, no, Jack! Daddy! You broke him!" She placed her head in her arms on the table and sobbed.

"Brad, how could you?" Janice asked.

He leaned down and picked up the broken pieces of Jack, setting them on the countertop.

"I'm so sorry, Emily. Daddy had a very bad day and it doesn't help when your mother doesn't do anything around here to help me. I'll get you another one and it will be ten times better than that one. Now, stop crying. Stop crying and eat your supper."

The three ate in silence. Tears continued to roll down Emily's cheeks and Janice's heart was in as many pieces as Jack was. After dinner, Janice told Emily to go ahead and finish her homework up in her bedroom. After Emily left the room, Janice started to clean up the splashed soup off the table and the wall. Brad got up off his chair, grabbed her arm and swung her around, hitting her head off the wall she had just cleaned. He wrapped his large hand around the front of her neck and pushed her head back, holding her in place. He glared into her eyes, moved into her with his face about an inch away and with a hiss, dripping with venom, said, "Don't you ever make me look bad in front of my daughter again." He let go of her neck, just long enough to backhand her face. In awe and confusion, Janice looked into his eyes as she touched her trembling hand to her sore and bloodied mouth. There was nothing but evil looking back at her. His eyes were cold, dark, and empty. He went to the refrigerator, grabbed a beer and plopped on the couch where he fell asleep for the night.

Janice woke up in the morning after very little sleep the night before. She tossed and turned all evening. Sometime in the night she heard Brad slowly creep up the stairs and enter their bedroom. She instantly shivered when he sat on the bed, marveling at how cold it just became. She pretended she was sleeping while he pulled off his shirt and pants and crawled in the bed beside her. She was very aware of the beer on his breath as he curled up to the back of her, his mouth on her cheek. His closeness made her skin crawl. She laid as still as she could and, eventually, he began to snore. She pulled her body away from his and clung to the edge of the mattress. Her mind was racing. A million "what-ifs", one right after another, entered her mind. "What-if he hurts Emily?", "What-if he tries to kill me?", "What-if he takes Emily away from me?", "What-if I leave and I can't make it on my own?", "What-if it's wrong to leave my husband?", "What-if I fail?" She then remembered her conversation with Kathy. Kathy explained that, when we "what if", we create anxiety through catastrophizing. She remembered that Kathy helped her to see all the ways she was strong and all the ways she had successfully addressed and solved problems before. She remembered Kathy telling her about the domestic violence shelter in the city and that all she needed to do was show up at the door. When Kathy first told her about the shelter, she thought there was no way she would ever go to a shelter. She didn't want anyone to know what was happening to her. And she didn't know any of those people. She probably wouldn't have anything in common with those people. But as she clung to the side of her mattress in a full-blown panic attack, she thought, of course I have something in common with them. I am them. I am a woman in a domestic violence situation. She found herself regretting not preparing a bag for herself and Emily as Kathy had suggested. She tried to calm her nerves and slow her thoughts, knowing that she was at the cusp of having to make some big decisions for herself and Emily. With that thought, she knew she better get some sleep, so she closed her eyes and visualized the gorgeous white cottage on the water her parents have in Florida. Through thoughts of warm, salty breezes and the lapping of water on the shore, she finally fell to rest.

Janice awoke to Brad's alarm going off. He slammed a heavy hand on the snooze button and rolled over nuzzling Janice's neck with his unshaven face and sharp-tongued mouth. He slid his hand up her leg and under her nightgown as she stiffened and tried to pull away from him.

"How about a little morning love before work baby?" He continued to run his mouth over her neck and pulled her over on her back.

"Brad, please, not this morning. Emily needs to get up soon for school and you need to get ready for work. How about we plan on having a special night together when you get home from work?" She knew this had angered him as darkness came across his eyes, his lips snarled over his teeth. She swore the room got cold again. He jumped out of the bed.

"Who do you think you are rejecting me. You're nothing but a lazy, fat bitch. I do everything for you and all you do is care about yourself." She slowly slid herself off the other side of the bed, trying not to look at him. "Look at you. You're disgusting. I don't know what's worse, your frizzy hair or your big fat ass that seems to get bigger every time I look at it. You honestly think you could get someone better than me? You honestly think anyone would want to be with you? Who would want a pig like you?"

She was enraged. She straightened her shoulders and looked him right in the eye and, with that, came an open-handed slap across her cheek. It would be the second time in a 24-hour period she tasted her own blood. He stormed off and went into the bathroom. She heard his evil laughter over the shower spray and she lowered herself back onto the mattress. A single tear left a streak over her pink, swollen cheek and through the blood coming from her lip. She reached up to wipe it off, wincing with her own delicate touch, and applied some quick foundation from the tube she kept on her stand by the bed. She, then, put on the best smile she could muster. She had a beautiful little girl sleeping like an angel in the room next door that needed to wake up and get ready for school.

As Janice and Emily were upstairs getting ready for the day, she heard the front door shut. Her body softened with relief, knowing Brad had left for work. She would make Emily her breakfast and take her to school and then come back home. She had much to do.

After Emily was dropped off at school with hugs and kisses and her favorite lunch, peanut butter and strawberry jelly, wrapped up with love in a brown bag, Janice returned home. She went straight upstairs and stripped off all her clothing. She went into the bathroom and stood in front of the long length mirror on the back of the door as she took every inch of her body in. She slid her hands up her legs and felt her own soft skin. She caressed the insides and the backs of her thighs that had turned soft and lumpy with cellulite. She then ran her hands over her hips and around her buttocks. She touched her stomach and took in the stretch marks where she carried her baby girl. She circled her breasts that weren't in the same place they used to be. She rubbed her hands up her neck and softly touched her sore, swollen cheek. She stared into her own eyes. They were tired and sad looking eyes. She reached up to touch her course auburn hair, realizing that it was frizzy. It used to be a long, glossy mane that landed at the middle of her back. She remembered Brad's words that morning, "Who would want you, anyway? Look at your frizzy hair." With that, she reached in the drawer beside her and pulled out a pair of scissors. She began chopping off chunks of old, frizzy hair. She could feel them landing on her breasts and stomach and gradually falling all around her feet. When she was left with a short, Pixi-like cut. She put the shears away and slowly walked out of the bathroom, leaving pieces of herself scattered on the floor.

Janice put on a new outfit and began pulling out two suitcases. She gathered enough clothes for herself and Emily. She also remembered some of the items Kathy had mentioned she should have prepared in a bag and, so she collected her medication which

43

included a newly refilled...thankfully...bottle of Xanax, her inhalers for her asthma and Emily's favorite flavored fever reducer, just in case. She gathered their birth certificates and social security cards. She grabbed her check book and some of the financial information regarding their family assets. And one last thing, Emily's Huggy Bear. She loaded up the car and with a big deep breath, she pulled away from the house and toward the address Kathy had provided. About half an hour later, Janice reached out her hand apprehensively to ring the chrome doorbell fastened to a building that looked just like all the other houses in the neighborhood. The door buzzed opened and a short, rounded lady with blonde curly hair and glasses smiled and simple said, "Welcome."

Janice found out the blonde, curly haired lady was Pattie. Pattie was the morning counselor who had been working at the shelter for over 10 years. After Pattie introduced herself to Janice, she walked her through the door of the office leading to the inside of the residential area. What was quiet in the office space was the opposite inside the residential area. It was bustling with women and young children. Women were laughing, a tv was playing in the corner of the living room and toys were all over the floor. Kathy began feeling overwhelmed with fear and started doubting her decision to come to the shelter. Pattie sensed Kathy's doubt, softly grabbed her arm and said, "It gets easier, Dear." She introduced Kathy to some of the women and then took her to the kitchen area. There in the kitchen, was a black woman in her fifties named Alicia and a thin, white woman with sandy blond hair in her forties whose name was Tina. The two women were elbow deep in a huge pile of collard greens. They were down to do the dinner chore tonight and promised the shelter ladies they would prepare greens and bacon from the abundance of greens that were donated last evening. They welcomed Janice and then promptly got back to work to prepare the delicious feast.

After completing some introductory paperwork and getting help from some of the girls to bring her and Emily's things up to their room, Janice tried to make it look as homey as she could. She perched Huggy Bear up on Emily's pillow and hung the picture of brightly colored pumpkins she had colored and had hanging on the refrigerator at home. Janice was terribly nervous about how Emily would respond to the fact that her mother would not be taking her home tonight but, instead, to an odd house full of strangers. Janice knew she didn't particularly like the prospects either, but she knew she had to do something. She knew that the violence at home was escalating and would just get worse if she stayed there.

It was finally time for school to get out, so Janice headed out to pick up Emily. As she sat waiting for her beautiful girl, Janice got increasingly nervous. Finally, Emily opened the door, full of smiles. She slid up into her seat and kissed her mom on the cheek.

"Hi, Sweetie, how was your day?"

"It was okay, Mom. What's wrong?"

"Honey, nothing is wrong, but we will be doing things a little different for a little while. Sweetie, we are going to be staying with some nice ladies for a little while. There's some kids there your age you will be able to play with."

"But why? I don't want to go anywhere but home. I want to go home and see Daddy, Mommy!"

46

"I know, Emily. But we can't go home right now."

"Is this because of Jack? It's all my fault, Mommy! I should have never asked to get him. I should have known Daddy would be mad. It's all my fault!"

Janice's heart broke to think her daughter blamed herself and wanting to have a pumpkin for Halloween for her parents' behavior. "No, Emily, you did absolutely nothing wrong. Mommy and Daddy are just having some problems right now. It will be okay. Come on, I want you to meet some of those nice ladies."

Emily was quiet and solemn that evening. The house was full of women and children and was chaotic with voices and laughter and the clinking of dishes and cookware. The television in the corner of the living room was playing at a high volume to an audience of teenagers. Janice and Emily went up to their room and Emily crawled up on her bed and wrapped her arms around Huggy Bear, tears rolling down her face. It took everything Janice could to not let her own tears break free. She put on a big smile, grabbed the colored pencils and coloring books she taken from home, and jumped on

Emily's bed, "Come on. Let's color."

The next morning, after many requests on Emily's part that they go home after school and Janice telling her it wasn't time yet, Janice dropped Emily off at school and met the domestic violence advocate at the court house. A Temporary Protection from Abuse order was granted to Janice that covered both herself and Emily. She felt a little better after that was accomplished. Next, she had to find a job to take care of herself and her daughter. She knew it wasn't going to be easy. Brad insisted that she not work. She now knows that was one of the ways he had control over her. Not only did she not have any of her own money, she had very limited contact with others, therefore, leaving her limited in folks who could help her or empower her. When they first moved from Florida up to the area so that Brad could take over managing his uncle's rental business, she tried to help him out. When he was busy all day at another office building or rental house, she would ask if she collect the rent. She looked forward to going to the different offices to get out and talk to other adults. She had met a few nice people and needed to feel connected to the outside world, even if it was somewhat superficial. At first,

Brad was agreeable to her collecting the rent for some of the office rentals if it didn't take away from what she needed to do at home, but that came to an abrupt stop after he dropped by one of the buildings after completing a project in one of the rental homes early. He caught Janice talking to a good-looking accountant. It was completely innocent, of course, but Brad was livid. He told her to go home immediately and he followed her while driving his car behind her. Once they were inside the house, he accused her of being a whore and wanting to sleep with all the men in the offices. He told her she was embarrassing herself because none of those men would ever want to be with her and she embarrassed him since she let herself go so badly. He insisted that she never go back into the rentals again and, ironically, the accountant Brad saw Janice talking to was denied a new contract after his year's lease was up. After that, Janice became dangerously isolated. She no longer worked and, seldom, did she have any opportunities to socialize for the last eight years unless it had something to do with Emily and her school.

The thought of finding a job was daunting for Janice. She didn't even have a resume. What would she even put on it? She had some experience in office work because she used to work for her dad in his office. Her dad was a Family Physician in Florida and her mom was a nurse. Her parents worked together in her dad's private practice for as long as she could remember. When she was in high school and after she graduated she helped her parents run the office. Her dream was to go to nursing school like her mom but then she met Brad. She fell fast and hard in love with Brad and he promised to love and take care of her forever. As they were dating, there became more and more complications with her parents. Brad would tell her that he didn't think they liked him. He would tell her that they treated him differently when she wasn't around and that he believed they thought he wasn't good enough for her. She asked her parents about this several times and, although they denied ever doing those things, they did start to express concern for her. Janice and her parents became more and more distanced and, eventually, Janice would get into a terrible fight with them and move out to live with Brad. Brad told her he thought they should have a fresh start where everything was new and exciting and full of possibilities, so they moved away from Florida and ended up in Pennsylvania, where Brad's uncle offered him the job running his rental business. Once they got up to Pennsylvania, Janice realized it was not any better than Florida. There were no more opportunities except for Brad's job and now she was away from the ocean and, most importantly, her parents and all the people who she cared about and who cared about her. Since they left on such bad terms, it was hard for her to call her mom and dad, but she missed them so much she couldn't take it. She was all alone and didn't know anybody. She met Brad's uncle Mike, but they didn't really seem to hit it off. Eventually she called her parents, expecting them to be angry and to tell her she made a terrible mistake, but they didn't do that at all. They told her they loved her more than anything in the world and that they would always be there for her, no matter what. Janice's mom's last words when they said their goodbyes were, "Don't forget, honey, you can always come home."

It wasn't but four months later that Emily would find out she was pregnant. Now, eight years later, she still lived in Pennsylvania. She hadn't seen her parents in a couple years since their last visit. She felt very alone and isolated. Brad continued to try to convince her that no one could really love her, including her friends and family. And it was hard to meet new friends when she's raising a child, has no job, and isn't allowed to go out alone without getting several phone calls wondering why she's not home yet. So, Janice felt like she was starting completely from scratch and she had to find a job, fast. She felt very overwhelmed and disillusioned. Pattie and Sylvia, the evening counselor, told her not to panic. They scheduled her to meet with a job counselor next week and referred her to a few job placement sites. They assured her that it would all work out in time. Kathy was also supporting her through this process and provided her with a few referrals. She was beginning to see that there were some caring people out there and that she didn't have to feel alone anymore. This thought comforted her. Maybe she could make it through this. With some help, maybe she could save herself and her daughter.

Chapter 6

It was the week of Halloween and Janice had a lot to do. She was helping the shelter women gather items from the donation room for the children to use as costumes for tomorrow's Trick or Treating. After that she had an appointment with Kathy and then she would go out again on the search for a job. She had an interview scheduled in the afternoon before she had to pick up Emily from school and then there was pumpkin carving at the shelter. The local greenhouse had contacted the shelter a week ago and asked if they could donate pumpkins for the children at the shelter. The staff was thrilled to accept their donations and had planned to pick up 12 pumpkins that day.

Janice was looking forward to seeing Kathy. Between ongoing voice messages from Brad and the fact that she still hasn't found a job, she really needed the support. She always felt stronger and empowered after her therapy sessions and she needed as much empowerment as she could get.

Janice and Kathy talked about her need to focus on self-care and caring for Emily. They explored her basic needs and how to fulfill those needs. They discussed self-esteem building and the importance of knowing that, by her mere existence, she was unique and special and "enough". She was good enough, smart enough, strong enough and, lovable enough. Janice knew she needed to start accepting herself just as she was. She needed to love herself, no matter how difficult it was for her to drown out all those old messages. After so many years of being away from people who cared about her and after being told repeatedly that she was ugly and worthless and unlovable, she began to believe those words were true.

Janice sat in Kathy's office and numerous memories flooded her. All the horrible things Brad had said to her, all the ways he hurt her, the look of disgust in his twisted-up face. She reached up and ran her hand through her short hair and shook her head as to stop the thoughts from coming. She could stop the effect those memories were having on her, slowly but surely. She would look for all the ways she was beautiful and special. She would remind herself each time those dreadful thoughts and memories would come up and, someday, they wouldn't come up so automatically. She had to start accepting herself for her and for Emily's sake.

As usual, Janice felt better after her session. She stopped by the cafe down the street to get a coffee before she headed out to a couple of stores she heard were hiring. She, then, her interview at a doctor's office on the way to Emily's school.

After her interview, Janice picked Emily up from school. She slid into the car with her backpack overflowing with papers. She noticed pages covered in pumpkins and ghosts and asked Emily if she was getting excited about Halloween. She simply shrugged her shoulders and quietly said, "I guess." Janice told Emily they found all kinds of neat things for their costumes to go Trick or Treating tomorrow.

Emily lowered her head and softly said, "Mom, I don't think I want to go. You and Daddy always take me Trick or Treating."

"I know, Honey. It's hard not seeing Daddy and getting to go with him this year."

"Then why won't you let us go home, Mommy? Why did you do

this to Daddy?"

"I know you don't understand Emily, but we had to go. Daddy and I were having problems and he was getting very angry."

"But what if you helped him more, like he said?"

"Sweetie, I will never be able to do enough. I hope someday you will understand. Please just know I love you more than anything in this world and I am doing what I think is best for you and myself"

Janice's heart was breaking in pieces again. How is she supposed to stay positive when her daughter is hurting so badly and is resenting her? Once again, Janice found herself doubting herself and her decision.

Once they arrived back at the shelter, the mother and daughter went into the residential area to see the dining room table lined with newspapers and pumpkins. Pattie, the shelter counselor, smiled from ear to ear, "Look what we got for you Emily." Emily looked up at her mom, her face turned red, her eyes filled with tears and she whispered, "Daddy broke Jack." She turned and ran up the stairs.

"Emily...." Janice took off after her.

"No," Pattie said, "let me go talk to her."

Janice lowered herself onto the couch, her hand covering her mouth. How is she ever going to make everything okay? Two of the shelter women sat down on the couch with her, one on each side. They both grabbed one of her hands and smiled warmly. "Hang in there. You'll get through this.

About an hour later, Pattie came down with Emily. Emily hugged Janice and told her mom she loved her. Janice held her tightly, kissed her cheek and told her sweet girl she loved her too.

"Do you think you want to try and carve another pumpkin?" Emily nodded her head and ran over to the table where the other children had already started. Sandy's daughter, Jill, invited Emily to sit with her and it wasn't long before pumpkin guts were slipping through the fingers of two giggling girls.

After the pumpkins were all carved, Pattie took the kids of various ages into the office where all the items the women pulled for Trick or Treating were waiting. As she helped them, along with two young volunteers, the women who had dinner chores were preparing a quick and simply dinner of chicken tenders and sweet potato fries. It had been a very long day and the excitement was just beginning for the children.

Emily and Jill finally decided their Trick or Treating costumes would be matching old ladies. They each wore a curly gray-haired wig with random rollers hanging off their heads. They were adorned with large pieces of costume jewelry including pearl bead necklaces and obnoxious looking broaches that were pinned to equally unattractive cardigans and pinned up polyester pants. After a couple hours of treading through crunchy leaves in the dark, going from house to house collecting yummy treats, the children and the adults were tired and ready to call it a night.

Chapter 7

Just as Janice and all the shelter women and children managed to

make in through and have an enjoyable experience Trick or Treating,

there were some folks that weren't feeling very enthusiastic about

Halloween at all.

Andy and Linda were distant and irritated with one another. They

continued to struggle with trying to feel more connected. Neither one

of them were happy with the lack of progress in their relationship.

Andy was angry with Linda for being so distant and not really

following through with the homework Kathy had given them. Linda

felt that Andy wasn't doing enough to engage with her or make her

feel special.

They both felt unfulfilled having another quiet and lonely

Halloween. They had a big bowl of candy ready at the door that

Andy had excitedly purchased for the big night. He picked up

several bags of candy since the stores started stocking the shelves for the big day, but he knew he would be the only one getting up and entertaining the visiting children. He didn't mind that so much because he loved children and always enjoyed spending time with the young ones but, lately, it just reminded him of how alone he was. It reminded him of how empty and meaningless his life felt. It hurt that Linda didn't participate in these events with him. He knew she would just be sitting in her chair with her nose in her book, like she did every day. She would have her nose in the book, because she couldn't stand the silence and the distance, herself.

In her own home, Kathy was alone with her porch light turned off, knowing Max would be going crazy and barking incessantly. She curled up in her hole on the couch, eating all the candy.

It turned out, however, that Kathy's night wasn't so uneventful after all. It turned out to be quite interesting.

After eating about a third of the candy and feeling half sick, her smartphone beeped, notifying her that she received a social media message. She was pleasantly surprised to see it was a message from Chase, one of her best friends from college. He was dating Nancy,

Kathy's roommate and best friend at the time and he, ultimately, would become one of her best friends as well. Nancy, Chase, and Kathy did everything together. Eventually, unfortunately, Nancy and Chase started doing more and more things on their own and Kathy was left behind. She and the couple ended up terminating their relationship before they all graduated from college and Nancy and Chase married and had a child. That was a painful and lonely time for Kathy and she grieved the loss of her friends for quite some time. Throughout the years after graduation attempts would be made on both sides to reconnect but distance created obstacles. Eventually Nancy and Chase would part ways after a tumultuous divorce. Thanks to social media, Kathy kept in touch with both Nancy and Chase but lost contact with Nancy all together. Chase and Kathy would randomly send each other a quick greeting or a picture one knew the other would like. The last time Kathy talked to Chase on messenger he told her he was remarrying but the marriage apparently only lasted one month.

Kathy responded to Chase's message Halloween night and they ended up chatting back and forth for hours. She was thrilled to hear from him and to remember all the funny things they did together nearly twenty-seven years ago when Kathy was eighteen years old. The conversation ended with a plan to reconnect in the following week. She was delighted to be speaking with her friend again and was pleasantly surprised when he told her he thought of her often. She was even more surprised that, after Halloween night, there would be a serious of additional texts to follow.

Chapter 8

The Scutellas had an appointment with Kathy the day after Halloween. Andy was looking forward to he and Linda having a chance to talk about the ongoing distance. He was also hoping to discuss some personal insights he had last night when he was handing out candy during Trick or Treating. He reminded Linda of the appointment and asked if she wanted to just meet him at Kathy's office or did she want him to come home after work and pick her up first. She stated she wasn't feeling well and wasn't sure she would be able to make the appointment. He was instantly disappointed in this and stated he really hoped she would go. She agreed to check in with him in the afternoon to see if she was feeling more up to it. Linda worked from home doing some freelance writing for various products, so she had plenty of time and flexibility, as a matter of fact, she was hardly working anymore at all. She was getting less requests for her work as time went by. Freelance writing wasn't what she wanted to do, but after her depression and anxiety continued to progress, it was about all she was able to do. She was writing a cooking column and an entertainment column for the local newspaper, but she couldn't keep up with the deadlines and demands. Her depression robbed her of her ability to focus and concentrate. She couldn't motivate herself enough to complete the columns as needed and she was always too exhausted and anxious to complete interviews. Her ultimate dream was to write a novel, but her depression robbed her of that as well. She could barely think, not alone be imaginative and creative. So, most of the time, she spent her days reading and sleeping.

During lunch time, Andy ran across the street and bought a sandwich and a chocolate milkshake. He called Linda at home to see how she was feeling. She groggily answered the phone and told him she had gone back to bed after he left, and she just woke up when he called. She felt too tired and sick to get up and get ready for the appointment. He became angry and told her if she didn't want to fix their relationship that was fine, but he wasn't going to keep going through this and he was just going to go to the appointment without her. He turned off his cell and shook his head. He was desperate. He resented her so much for not doing anything to fix herself or the relationship. He was depressed and ill too, but he still had to get up every day and work and pretend everything was fine. He didn't get to stay home, under the blankets not doing anything. The longer this went on, the more he wondered why he even wanted to try to fix the marriage. This wasn't the life he wanted for himself. He didn't know how much more he could take. He continued to grow wearier and discouraged. Was their relationship even reparable at this point?

After a very long and exhausting afternoon of patients, Andy made his way to Kathy's office. She noted he was alone and he rolled his eyes, stating Linda was under the weather and didn't want to come. Kathy listened to him angrily describe what happened that day and she stated it sounded like he was feeling hopeless and helpless regarding his marriage. He nodded and reached for a tissue on the side of the table. The two talked about coping with a spouse with depression and she suggested the couple invest in a popular book for spouses coping with their depressed loved one. Kathy believed this may be a good resource for the couple as they both struggled with depressed mood.

Kathy asked Andy if he would like to talk about anything else since he came alone. He told her about last night's Trick or Treating. She found her own stomach cramp a little, thinking about the candy she had eaten the night before. He shared with her that he struggled with feeling worthless and meaningless. Kathy stated she was interested in the fact that the man sitting before her who saved people for a living would feel he had no purpose or meaning. She wondered out loud what a meaningful life would look like for Andy. He shared with her that he knew he was a good doctor but there was still something missing. While giving candy out last night, Andy realized how much he lit up around children. He was coming to understand that the fact he and Linda never had children affected him much more than he realized. He wanted a family. He wanted children. He told Kathy about how he and Linda had tried having children a few years ago and they were never able to get pregnant. They figured they would always have time to pursue it more seriously later. Their relationship became more and more difficult and, he guessed, the idea of children just got put on the back burner.

Then, about a year ago, Linda had problems with terrible fibroids in her uterus and had to have a hysterectomy. The prospect of having children was never discussed again. He told Kathy that there were two contributing factors on his part. One, he didn't want to start an argument with Janet or make her feel bad. He didn't want her to think he blamed her because she had to have the hysterectomy. He knew their problems were more complicated and existed prior to her health issues. Two, he was always so busy and preoccupied that, by time he got home, he couldn't slow down his brain enough to have a decent conversation with Linda. Kathy pointed out that he needed to address how to better manage that problem because that was part of Linda's complaint, that she felt distanced and disconnected from him. She had reported that he never talked to her. Kathy asked Andy if there was a way for him to address that problem. She wondered if he could do something after work that would help him to transition from Andy, the doctor to Andy, the husband. She asked him if there was ever a time when he could feel a sense of calm and peace in the past. He shook his head and quietly said, "church". He further explained that his father used to be a preacher and Andy remembered setting in the pew beside his mom, feeling peaceful and safe. He remembers this clearly because it was one of the very few times he ever felt peaceful and safe within his family. His family was very chaotic, addictive, and emotionally unwell. Andy then told Kathy that he would eventually doubt there was a God and never returned to the church again. Kathy wondered if he were to go to the church on times when they were not congregating if he might be able to obtain that sense of peace again. He was intrigued by this idea and was willing to give it a try. They developed an action plan that one day between the office visit and his next appointment, he would go to the church after work and allow himself to relax and meditate in the pew for about twenty minutes before going home.

Kathy also asked Andy how he felt about talking to Linda about his revelations from last night and his feeling about children. He stated he would consider the possibility. Kathy wondered if there was any other way he would consider fulfilling this need to have children and asked him to consider how he could meet that need in the future. With his assigned homework, Kathy and Andy rescheduled a follow up appointment, hoping Linda would attend the next one, and ended their session for the day.

Andy was Kathy's last client for the day, so she went around the office turning off all the lights and gathering her briefcase. She hadn't heard from her brother in a couple weeks and he hadn't responded to any of her texts. She sent another message earlier in the morning and he never responded to that one either. That wasn't unlike him to not respond but she was starting to get concerned about him since it had been so long since they last spoke. She needed to see for herself if he was ok.

Just as Kathy was getting into her vehicle to go see Will her phone beeped, notifying her she had a message. It would turn out there were two messages on her phone. The most recent one that just came through was from Will, "I'm at work. Too busy." and the second one must had come through earlier in the day. It was from Chase, "I'm curious. Have you ever thought about us dating? BTW, I have."

Kathy instantly felt both panic and excitement in response to Chase's disclosure. She found herself questioning why his message caused her to have such a mixed reaction. She thought she should be happy that he just shared interest in her. And she certainly was thrilled that this man who was once her close friend and "the boy" had an interest in her. But she wasn't sure she was willing to put herself in such a vulnerable position again, especially when something just didn't feel right to her. Kathy had become very comfortable being a single, independent forty-five-year-old and she enjoyed the life she made for herself. Admittedly, however, despite her instincts telling her something didn't feel entirely right, the idea of talking to Chase was somewhat alluring. She might be playing with fire but, she was tempted to play, nonetheless. Perhaps she could just see how it goes.

Kathy found herself writing a quick message to Will, "Let me know when we can get together", picked up pizza and then spent several hours setting on her couch with Max, munching on slices of thin, cheesy heaven, and messaging Chase.

More and more, their conversations were getting intimate and personal. They talked about their days and shared hopes and dreams about future goals, traveling, family, companionship and what they expected in their lives as they aged.

"If you were here right now," Chase said, "I could cook for you and we could cuddle in front of the fireplace and watch movies. Maybe you could come and stay a weekend."

"That would be great," Kathy said, although secretly afraid of how he would react to her when he saw how much weight she had gained since they knew each other in college but she was too embarrassed to share her fears with him. He had suggested a get together before, but she found a reason to delay the discussion. She knew she needed to let the fear go and just be herself. If he lost interest in her, he wasn't worth the effort anyway. So, Kathy was trying to open to the idea of meeting with him in the future. This was a new time in her life and she was trying to appreciate herself and her body in new ways.

Kathy didn't have many men in her life. Sure, she had her crushes in high school but never had a high school boyfriend. Turns out, when you are the fat, shy, poor daughter of an alcoholic, you don't have a lot of young boys knocking at your door. Was that because Kathy was fat or shy or poor? Absolutely not! None of the above, really. It was her own self-fulfilling prophecy. It was because she believed she wasn't worthy of having a boyfriend. She told herself she wasn't good enough and would never really put herself out there. It would take her until she was much older to understand that it wasn't so much what others had thought of her, it was what she thought of herself.

As a young girl, Kathy would never have a first date. In high school, on Valentine's Day, the students had Carnation Day where they would buy each other carnations. Kathy would be the one without a flower when most of the students would be carrying around several or wearing them pinned proudly on their chests as evidence that they were special and lovable. Kathy had no such evidence of her own. And when prom time came, there was no buildup of excitement looking for the perfect dress that would bring admiring glances of others. She spent the night at home, eating pizza with her family, and watching television.

When Kathy went away to college she had a few crushes as well, still too shy to interact with the boys. Still too self-conscious of her weight, which, by the way, she gained a lot more than the freshman 15. Before it was all said and done, it was more like the freshman 60.

It wouldn't be until after her college years that she started to come into her own as a young woman. She began to open a little and interact with men enough to land a few socially awkward dates that led to some, even more, awkward sexual experiences. But those men never cared about her. They were relationships of convenience. She gave herself sexually to them but could never trust them to give them anything more. Nor did they want it. They didn't want her.

Chapter 9

Andy sat stiffly in the church pew. He would never have entered

those doors if he hadn't thought maybe Kathy had a good idea. No

matter what he believed or didn't believe at this point, the church

was always a place of peace for him and he needed to be willing to

do whatever he could to lower his own stress levels.

As he sat in the pew, trying to relax and take nice, slow breaths,

the pastor and a few other folks began to mill around the stage,

pulling out large, worn boxes of decorations and set materials. A few

young children were involved with this activity and were clearly

excited as they discussed who would get the best parts in the

upcoming holiday play.

Andy became distracted by watching the bustle before him. He

was watching a young boy about the age of eight years old beam with pride as he pulled out a shepherd's staff and walked across the stage. Just then the pastor of the church walked down the aisle toward Andy. "I'm so sorry. The children were promised they could go through some of the pieces for the play and begin pulling out materials and costumes for rehearsal. It gets them out of the homes and shelters and gives them something to look forward to." Andy was curious what the pastor meant by homes and shelters. Pastor Dominic explained that every year, the various foster children and children in community services were invited to the church to participate in the holiday play. It was an outreach program that Pastor Dominic initiated about 5 years ago and was a big success. As the pastor described the program to Andy he noticed that Andy, who initially sat in the pew looking solemn and distressed, now seemed to light up with interest. The pastor then asked Andy if he would like to help with this year's play. He stated they needed more volunteers and could use any extra help they could get. Andy instantly began to decline but then looked up at the stage at the children and couldn't help but notice that boy trying so hard to play the part. It reminded him of himself when he was a young boy, trying desperately to make his parents proud. All he wanted was to make them happy. He would learn in time that he would never be able to accomplish that task as his parents were quite unwell. He saw that same need and determination to prove something in that young boy's face. With that recognition, Andy nodded his head, "Yes. I think I would like to volunteer."

Andy woke up in the morning feeling excited about the day. He acknowledged that something was different with him. He would typically wake up dreading the long, hard day ahead but all he could think of this morning was his session with Kathy and then the meeting at 6:30 at the church for all the volunteers and participants in the play. He couldn't wait to tell Kathy about the church visit and his volunteering to help at the play. It wasn't exactly what she had in mind, but he knew she would be thrilled for him. He was really enjoying meeting with Kathy alone. She was helping him to see that he was in more control over his own fulfillment and happiness than he originally thought he was. She was helping him to understand that the way he reacted to his life had a lot to do with the way he thought about his life. This little bit of knowledge was giving him more hope than he had ever experienced in his entire life. He may be feeling lost and worried about his relationship, but he was beginning to believe he could, at least, start being a more whole and fulfilled person which would, hopefully, lead to him being an overall better person and spouse.

And, as far as his excitement about the play, he didn't know exactly what it was, but he got the feeling it was going to be something great. Maybe just getting his mind off all the stressors at work and home would do him a world of good. This, he learned, was called being mindful. If he got into the flow of doing something exciting and pleasurable that would give him a break from all his worries, that would be exactly what he needed. Then, maybe, the worries would be more manageable when he wasn't so overwhelmed.

Andy's day did go quickly and, before he knew it, he was sitting in Kathy's office telling her about the church experience and his volunteering. He was right. She was thrilled for him. She also was pleased to hear about Pastor Dom's program because she felt it may be a resource for some of her other folks worth considering.

After his session, Andy stopped to get a sandwich then headed over to the church. It was bustling with excitement and he felt at home amongst the others that would be participating. Pastor Dom shared the theme of the play was going to be the Christmas Story of baby Jesus's birth. He informed them the children's rehearsals would be starting this week. After introductions, the volunteer groups were developed. Andy volunteered to help with rehearsals so that he could work with the children directly. After therapy helped him to realize he struggled with a sense of worthlessness and meaninglessness and the fact he and Linda never had kids triggered these feelings within him, it seemed like the perfect opportunity to start finding new ways to fulfill himself and address those feelings.

After the meeting was over and everyone was dismissed, Andy looked up on the stage to see the same little boy form the other day walking around with the shepherd's staff. He asked the small, thin boy, "Getting a head start on rehearsals?"

The boy smiled and with a grin from ear to ear stated, "Yes, sir! I just must get the role of Joseph! It's my ticket out of foster care."

Andy was very interested in this statement. "Foster care?", he asked the young boy.

"Oh, yes! You see my mom gave me away a couple of years ago and I've been staying with my Gramma Wilcox since then. But my best friend, Jimmy Henderson, says he heard his mom and dad talking a while ago when he was in bed. He said they were saying they wanted to adopt another boy. He was mad at first but then he told me maybe they would adopt me and then we could be brothers and we could all be a family. They're the Hendersons. Charlie Henderson. Doesn't that sound like the perfect name? Charlie Henderson!"

Andy felt so bad and his heart melted for the eager little boy. He smiled softly, meeting the boy's eyes and said, "Charlie Henderson sounds like a very nice name, indeed. But what if there's someone else out there who would love to adopt you? Maybe you will be Charlie Smith or Charlie Adams?"

Shaking his head, vigorously, "No! There is no one else out there that wants me. I've tried and tried to be lovable enough, good enough. The only way this will work for me is if Jim can convince them. I've done good on my grades this year. I've stayed out of trouble. I haven't missed my curfew once. And best of all, Jim said he will get his parents to come to the play if I can get the lead role. That will, for sure, be when I convince them that I can be the boy they adopt."

Quite concerned to hear how much weight the little fellow was putting on himself, Andy, grabbed a script and said, "Well, maybe we can talk more about that later, but it sounds like we have some rehearsing to do. I'm Andy, by the way."

He reached out to shake the young fellow's hand, "I'm Charlie. Charlie Wilcox...for now."

Andy patted the back of the sandy haired boy with freckles, "Well Charlie Wilcox, I am very pleased to meet you. Now let's get rehearsing."

Chapter 10

Kathy was looking forward to going into the office today. She was

wondering how Janice and Emily were adjusting to communal

living. She knew it came with some challenges, but they were safe

and getting the help, they needed.

Before she headed to the office, however, Kathy wanted to stop

by the church and see if there was any literature she could give out

about the community program and the upcoming play. It had been a

long time since Kathy had been in a church and she was hoping she

could just run in and out quickly before she had to meet with Janice.

She found her way to the church and parked on the street in front

of the entrance of the building. She squeezed out from behind the

steering wheel and walked the small distance to the door. When she

entered the church, she paused to catch her breath and take in the

sights and sounds. It was quite dim with candles lit up on both sides

of the small room. It was big enough to hold three rows of 8 pews. A chandelier hung from the center of the room with several whirling

fans hanging down from the ceiling. There was a stage up front that

appeared large for the overall size of the room. An old wooden piano

sat on the far-right side of the stage.

Kathy felt herself becoming a bit sick to her stomach, so she slid

herself into the pew beside her. Being back inside a church was

bringing up memories, long ago stuffed in the corners of her mind,

and including the one from when she was about ten years old and

living with her dad. They didn't typically go to church but, her dad,

George, always insisted on attending midnight mass for Christmas

Eve. He was raised Catholic and, Kathy guessed, attending mass was

his way of staying connected to his own family traditions. The

problem was he would always be drunk off his ass by the time

midnight ever arrived. George and Kathy would walk to the church,

since he often didn't have a car. Arriving late, as usual, the father-

daughter duo would enter the giant ornate doors leading into the

cathedral and disrupt the beginning of service. The enormous room

filled with several rows of pews, containing, what felt to Kathy like

the entire town would become dead silent while everyone turned to stare at Kathy and George. She felt like she didn't belong there, and everybody seemed big and scary and intimidating. She felt alone, standing there beside her father who was never in the position of saving and protecting her. Kathy recalled, one particular time, she wanted to turn around and run out of the building but, instead, George started down the main aisle of pews, staggering and stumbling over himself. He was uninhibited with a loud voice and slurred speech, too intoxicated to understand how inappropriate talking was at the time.

"Let's set here, Kathy."

"Shhh, Dad." Kathy said, mortified that everyone was staring at them.

"Don't shhh me, Kathy. Jesus Christ! What's your problem?"

"I'm sorry, Dad. It's okay. This is a good place to set." Kathy whispered and grabbed his arm, pulling him into the pew.

Kathy couldn't get herself to look around the room. She knew there were people she knew in there. She knew her classmates were there. She knew what they must be thinking and saying. She just kept her head down, her chubby cheeks feeling crimson with pain and embarrassment, and begged that he just shut the hell up until they got out of there. She wondered if she would go to hell for praying to God to make her dad shut the hell up. Her stomach churned, her head pounded, and her heart broke. At some point in the service, a boy with a violent looking scar that stretched across his bald head from ear to ear, waved incense around the room that burned her nostrils, seared gruesome images into her brain, and made her sick.

After mass, not looking at anyone, Kathy drug her father out of the building telling him she was sick. Having been there a while, he was a little steadier on his feet.

"I'm sorry I yelled at you, Kathy.

"It's okay, Dad. Let's just get home."

"Tomorrow, I promise to make it up to you. I'll get you one of those big sodas you like. Okay? How does that sound?"

"Sounds good, Dad."

The next day, George gathered all his loose change together, so he could get Kathy her "don't be mad at me" drink. They walked all the way to town to the convenient store, so she could get her soda which consisted of a 32-ounce cup filled to the top with ice and about 5 different sodas all mixed together in the attempts to make the perfect soda, sweet and sticky and full of flavor. She felt better from the previous night's debacle just tasting the bubbly goodness. She clung to her "big gulp" with both hands, holding it tightly to her chest and sucking from the long straw. George paid for the soda and the two exited the store and headed back home.

Kathy noticed her shoe lace was untied and asked George to hold her drink, so she could tie her shoe. As she handed him the slippery cup that she was holding with both hands, it slipped out of his hand and burst open, spilling the sweet peace offering all over the sidewalk and her shoes.

"Oh, no, Dad." It was all gone.

"Oh, no, Kathy. I'm so sorry. I'm such a fuck up." He bent down and picked up the empty container, holding it with one hand and digging through his pocket with the other hand. He knew he didn't have any more money to buy her another one but dug anyway, hoping something would appear.

She knew he didn't have any more money too and it broke her heart that he was so desperately digging in his pockets for something, anything to make it all better. She gripped his arm, "It's okay, Dad. I really had enough. I don't think I made it right anyway. We can get another one some other day. I need to add more lemon lime soda and less cola the next time. Plus, I'm full of guzzling so much of it, all at once, before it spilled."

"You sure? We will get you another one later and that one will be so much better."

"Okay, thanks, Dad. You're right. The next one will be the best."

As they walked home, Kathy felt some relief that her father seemed to stop loathing himself for dropping her drink, but, damn it, she sure wanted that soda. It was the best one she had made yet.

Shaking away her memory, Kathy felt a gentle hand on her shoulder, "Ma'am? Ma'am? Are you okay?"

"Oh, yes, thank you. I'm sorry. I was just enjoying the quiet and peaceful atmosphere. It's quite lovely in here." Both Kathy and the Pastor were aware of the tears streaming down her cheeks as she quickly tried to brush them away.

"Thank you. I'm Pastor Dom. Is this your first time in our church?"

"Oh, Pastor Dom. You're just the person I was looking for. Yes. It is my first time here. I dropped by to see if you have any literature or materials on your community program and the play. I'm a therapist in private practice in the community and have some folks I think would benefit from participating."

After a few more pleasantries, an armful of flyers, and an invitation to return to the church anytime Kathy would like, she left the church and hurried to the office, fearing she was going to be late for her appointment with Janice.

Thankfully, Janice arrived a few minutes late as she had just finished up with an interview at the cafe down the street. She shared with Kathy that she was really worried about finding a job. She did go to the job placement site that she was referred to and they helped her get a resume completed. She knew it wasn't great because of the long gaps in between but there was nothing more she could do. She was really hoping to get an office job but the longer it took, the further away that dream became. She would really love to have an office job in an office like Kathy's. She always liked working directly with people. Kathy reminded her it is a process and to not give up. She reminded her to believe that she would find something she really liked, if not right away, in the future. She knew she had to take what she could for now and then maybe that dream job would come someday.

Janice shared with Kathy that Emily has been becoming increasingly frustrated with living in the shelter. She had been asking to see or talk to her dad. Janice tried to explain how the Protection from Abuse order worked but Emily would just get angry and tell Janice she wished she would never have gotten the stupid thing. Janice knew how much it hurt Emily to not see her father and she felt so guilty to be keeping her away from him. She knew she had to keep them safe, but it broke her heart to see Emily sad. She knew she just didn't understand the seriousness of their situation. To top it off, she received a voice mail earlier that week from Brad begging her to come back with Emily. He told her he missed her and Emily so much and he promised he would never do anything to hurt her again. Janice felt her reserve weaken when she heard his voice on the other end. He sounded so sincere and lost without them. Was she making a mistake?

Kathy remembered talking to Andy about Pastor Dom's program and wondered if it would help Janice and Emily to have something fun to work on and look forward to. She told Janice all about the upcoming play and the community based program. Ironically enough, Janice stated, the shelter staff just told the ladies in shelter all about the program and told them they would hang a signup sheet on the wall if anyone would like to participate and needed bussed to the church.

At the time, Janice didn't give it a single thought. But as Kathy told her about it, she began to see it as a potential activity for her and Emily to do together and to get their minds off all the stress they were going through.

Chapter 11

With an agreement from Janice to see if Emily would be interested in the play, the two women scheduled for a follow up appointment and were saying their goodbyes when a knock on the office door interrupted them. "Kathy? Are you in there?"

"Oh, yes, Sam, I'll be right with you. I'm just finishing up."

"Okay. I didn't know if you had anyone in there. Hello," he said, pushing his arm through the small crack and waving at whomever might be in the office.

"Hello," Janice returned the greeting, giggling and looking at Kathy with surprise and amusement.

Kathy walked Janice out to the lobby where Sam was setting cross legged in one of the big chairs, scratching crazily on his sketch pad.

"Sorry about that. I've never seen you here before. Are you new here?" Sam asked Janice. "You'll like Kathy," he said, "She's a real bad ass."

Janice laughed out loud. "I do like her very much. Have a good day."

"Sam," Kathy said, "Come on back."

"She was really hot," Sam said, "You should give me her number."

"You know I can't do that, Sam. You're full of it today, aren't you? Did your mom bring you?" Kathy asked.

He nodded, "Yeah. I know. I'm a little manic today."

"A little?" Kathy though to herself.

Kicking off his shoes, Sam plopped into the chair across from Kathy and sat cross legged again. "I haven't slept in, I don't know, like 3 days, Dude. I had this huge inspiration and have been on a painting frenzy. I just finished the piece this morning. I wanted to bring it in to show you but it's still wet."

"I'm curious what your inspiration was," Kathy asked Sam.

"You," he said, "Well, not you, but something you said. You told me I was a self-fulfilling prophecy. That I wanted to be important and special but because I'm afraid I will just be rejected, I make myself inaccessible and unapproachable. Then I feel lonely and shitty and, then, drink and shoot up to deal with the loneliness. I'm starting to believe, through your help, slowly but surely, that I may already be those things I so desperately want."

Sam took his gray pin striped beret off his head and twirled it madly between his hands. "I'm thinking I'd like to get my shit together and start teaching art. Make a difference, you know? Teach people how to express themselves through art."

"How would that make you feel to be clean and to be able to use your gift to help other people?"

"Like I matter. Like I'm worthy. You know what I mean?"

"Sounds beautiful," Kathy nodded and smiled, "What do you think you would need to do to start moving yourself in the direction of this goal?"

Sam got up out of his chair, scratching his head and pacing the small floor of the office in his stocking feet for a few seconds and then sat down, once again, in his chair, his hair sticking out all over his head.

With his head lowered, he ran his hand through his black, glossy hair. Kathy noticed his hands were splattered in a mirage of colors that translated into an odd greenish purple. He let out a long sigh, lifted his head to look Kathy in the eyes, then shrugged and said, "I have to get clean. I have to go back into rehab."

Kathy looked right back into his eyes and nodded. "Who's going to call?" she asked.

He reached into his back pocket pulling out his cell phone. After finding the dual diagnosis facility he attended the last time in his contacts list, he pushed the little green phone and started his new path to sobriety. After planning with the caseworker to meet within the hour, he hung up his phone and asked Kathy as he slid his shoes back on, "There. Are you happy now?"

"I'm proud of you for making a courageous decision. I believe in you, Sam."

"Yeah, yeah," he said, hugging her, "I'll write you and let you know how it is going."

Kathy had him sign a Release of Information form, so she could speak with the facility staff and vice versa. She would not see Sam for a while since, after he completed his inpatient work, he would most likely be discharged into an outpatient dual diagnosis treatment.

After the paperwork was completed, Kathy walked Sam out to the lobby. She watched him walk away and toward his mom's car. As he slipped his beret and sunglasses back on, he disappeared into the sunlight.

She wondered if this time would be any different.

Chapter 12

Back at the shelter, Janice asked Emily if she would be interested in participating in the play. Emily seemed excited about participating. Janice hoped that Emily keeping busy with the play really would be an effective coping strategy for her while she and Janice continued their stay at the shelter. Emily told Janice, Jill, her new friend at the shelter, asked her to audition for the play with her. It was settled then. They put their names on the signup sheet to be bussed with the other ladies. They still could use more participants and there was another meeting next week.

Janice was pleased that Emily was looking forward to working on the play. She knew it would do them both good. Before she turned her bedside lamp out for the night, she checked her phone one more time. Brad had left another message. Her temples throbbed, and her throat tightened. She took in a deep breath and left out a long sigh. The tension let up a little, so she closed her eyes, slid far under the blankets and breathed deep, slow breaths: in for a count of 4, hold for a count of 7, and out for a count of 8.

She must have dozed off, but she awoke around one o'clock in the morning in a full sweat. She had a nightmare that Brad was following here and, no matter which way she went, she couldn't get away from him. No matter how much she ran, he was always there.

She shook her head as to remove the thoughts of her dream and wondered just how close to reality that nightmare was going to be. Would she ever really be free of him?

Janice got out from under the covers and slid her robe and slippers on. She snuck downstairs and noticed the kitchen light was on. As she got close to the doorway, she heard Alicia talking quietly on her cell phone while sipping a cup of tea. She heard Alicia say, "I can't come home. You keep telling me you are going to change, and you never do. I love you too Calvin, but that's not enough. I can't keep going through this." When she seen Janice in the doorway, she said, "I'm hanging up now, Calvin. Please leave me alone."

Janice made a full entrance, smiled sideways at Alicia, "You too, huh?" She ran the water in an old coffee mug and put it in the microwave as she pulled out a chamomile tea bag from the cupboard.

"Your old man bothering you, Janice?"

Janice steeped her tea bag in the hot water. "He's left me a couple messages. I didn't listen to the last one. He's asking me to come home. He says he loves me and won't hurt me anymore."

Alicia started shaking her head, "Oh, no, girl. Don't go believing that baloney. That's what they always say. Then they go right back to the same old shit. And, for that matter, sometimes it's even worse than when you left cause then they think they can get away with it."

Janice remembered Pattie and Sylvia telling her that women may go back to their abusers many times before they totally get away all together. They said something like the average number of times a woman will leave her abuser is approximately 7 times. They taught her about the Cycle of Violence and that, although it may not be quite that cyclical after all, there is usually a honeymoon phase where the abuser is loving and giving and promises to change. Then the tension begins to build again, and the abuse recurs. Sometimes there's not even much time in between these "phases". Janice had to keep reminding herself of these facts about domestic violence, especially when she started to feel guilty about taking Emily away from her dad, bad for hurting Brad's feeling, and missing her home. Sometimes she wondered if it would just be easier to have stayed, knowing what to expect for the most part, rather than facing all these challenges and hardships and feeling so lost and alone. What if he was right? What if she couldn't make it on her own? What if no one could ever love her?

She didn't even realize she asked that question out loud until she saw Alicia's jaw drop and her eyebrows raise as high as they could possibly go, "Girl! Don't you ever say that. That's just his bullshit to make you feel bad about yourself. You are so sweet and nice and you're a good mom, too. You hold that head up and know you are worthy of love. Don't be like me. I'm tired, girl. I've done left my Calvin more times than I can count. Now, here I sit, 55 years old and still haven't learned my lesson." Alicia looked away, shaking her head. "Hey, I got something for you, girl. You wait right here." Janice thought about poor Alicia. She was such a nice lady and she deserved to know she was worthy of good, healthy love too. When Alicia returned, she had a big smile on her face. She grabbed Janice's hand, slipped something in it and lifted it up to her mouth where she softly kissed her knuckles. "You keep this safe now girl. Never lose it." Janice opened her hand to see a small heart shaped keychain. On one side, the words, "You are loved", was etched on the front. A tear slipped down Janice's cheek and she looked up to meet Alicia's tearful golden eyes. They didn't need to say another word. They wrapped their arms around each other and held on tight. After a few minutes, they smiled at each other, put their cups in the sink and went on their separate ways to bed. A deep, loving and lifelong friendship had just been formed. Too bad it would be short lived.

Chapter 13

Janice was feeling tired and disillusioned. After Brad's late-night call and her emotional tea with Alicia, she struggled to get to sleep. After what seemed to be only a couple of hours of sleep, the alarm went off. She got up to get Emily ready for the day and off to school. After dropping Emily off, Janet spent a couple of hours at the job center and then went back to shelter. She had bathroom chore today which she was not looking forward to. Cleaning the bathroom at her house with her small family was disgusting enough, not alone four bathrooms that were being used by over twenty people. She always tried to avoid the bathrooms when they passed around the chore sheet at Sunday night house meetings but this last Sunday she received the chore sheet last and that was all that was left. Everybody else was trying to avoid bathroom duty as well.

After scrubbing the toilets, sinks and showers, Janice swept and mopped the floors. By time she was done she was sweating buckets, so she grabbed a quick shower before having to pick up Emily. They had their first meeting at the church for the play and Emily and Jill

had been talking about it for the last couple of days.

Janice noticed Emily was quiet after school. She was concerned,

thinking maybe Emily was no longer interested in participating in

the play, but Emily assured her mother she was looking forward to

going to the meeting that night. The problem was, Emily did

something that she knew her mother would not be happy about. Last

night, Emily knew her dad left a message on her mom's phone

because she seen her mom get upset and tearful after the phone rang.

When her mom got out of bed and went downstairs, Emily listened

to the message her dad left. He sounded so sad and she just didn't

understand why her mom was hurting him. She pushed the redial

button and heard her dad's voice come over the phone. Emily

instantly felt bad and wanted to hang up, but she heard her dad say,

"Hello? Janice? Anyone there?"

She answered, "Hi, Daddy. It's me, Emily."

"Where are you?" he asked.

"I don't know," Emily answered truthfully.

"What do you mean you don't know? Did your mom tell you to lie to me?" he asked his little girl with anger in his voice.

"No. She doesn't know I called you," Emily added, feeling the need to defend her mother.

"Well, what's the address, Emily? Can't you see the address? Are you staying with a man? Is your mother seeing another man? Tell me who she's with, Emily," he continued to only show an interest in locating Janice.

"No, Daddy. We are staying with a bunch of other people. I just missed you and wanted to tell you I'm going to be in a play, so you can come and see me," Emily stated, just wanting her father to show some interest in her.

"Tell me when and where it's going to be. I'll be there, and you make sure to tell your mother she's not going to get away with this," Brad hungrily awaited the information he needed to get his hands on Janice.

"It's December 10th at the red church on the way to the park."

"Okay. You better believe I'll be there," Brad concluded.

"I can't wait to see ....," Emily stopped talking when she heard her father hang up the phone. He was gone. Just like that. He didn't even seem like he missed her or interested in her. He didn't seem like he cared about the play either. It was if he only had one thing on his mind...her mother. She began to feel terrible that she had called him and thought she did something very bad. Should she tell her mom and risk getting in trouble? Maybe she would think about it and decide what to do later.

After having dinner at the shelter, Kathy and Emily, Sandy and Jill, and Melissa and her son, Jeff, all piled in the van. Emily and Jill had enough excitement for the whole group. Janice was tired and really didn't feel like going to the church but knew it was important for Emily. Sandy and Melissa weren't looking very enthusiastic either.

Pastor Dom separated the volunteers and the prospective actors into two different groups. He introduced Dr. Scutella and Mr. English, the two volunteer rehearsal coaches, and asked the actors to go with them to the recreation room to get scripts and talk about rehearsals. The remaining volunteers were divided into different categories. Emily and Jill went off with Dr. Scutella and Mr. English and Kathy, Jill, Melissa and Jeff were all chosen for different volunteer positions. Kathy was whisked away with costumes when she disclosed she liked to sew. Sandy and Melissa were sent over into makeup and Jeff went over to set building. It was a whirlwind of activity and Janice was surprised to see how quickly the two hours passed.

Dr. Scutella brought Emily back to Janice and told her young Emily was quite the talented actress. Emily beamed with pride. She told her mom she wanted to audition for the role of Mary.

"That's a very demanding role, Emily."

"I know Mom, but I can do it. Dr. Scutella told me he would help me rehearse Thursday night if you can bring me to the church. There's this really nice boy, Charlie who is auditioning for Joseph and Dr. Scutella said he could help us both rehearse together."

"Well, if it's okay with Dr. Scutella, I'll make sure you get here

Thursday. I know you can do anything you set your mind to."

Dr. Scutella seemed as thrilled that Janice gave her permission as Emily was. "That's wonderful. It would be my pleasure. You can call me Andy by the way."

After introductions, they all agreed to meet at the church Thursday at 7:00. The rest of the shelter folks met up with Kathy and Emily and they piled back on the bus back to shelter.

Emily and Jill giggled the whole way back to shelter which was fine by Janice. She was too busy worrying about how she was possibly going to get a job, not alone one that would be flexible enough to get Emily to her extra rehearsals. She also worried that Christmas would be here before she knew it and she still didn't have any money to get them on their feet, not alone, have a nice Christmas. Maybe she and Emily should just go back home. Brad and Janice always made sure Emily had a wonderful Christmas. Once again, she would be letting her baby girl down.

Andy was excited as well. He drove the short ride home, looking forward to telling Linda about his evening. He wondered if she would like to go with him and planned to ask her when he got home. He was very aware that, even though his day was long and exhausting, he felt full of energy. He couldn't believe how much he was enjoying himself.

He pulled up to the house and into the garage. When he entered the kitchen from the garage he was disappointed to see the house lights were turned off and Janet was already in bed. Suddenly, the house seemed terribly dark and empty.

Andy was hungry, so he flipped the kitchen light on and checked out the refrigerator. There was nothing to eat so he took a glass out of the kitchen cupboard and poured a small amount of milk into the glass. He sat at the table in silence for about an hour and then polished off the rest of his milk. He noticed, despite the milk, he still felt empty inside. He wondered if anything in his home could satiate his needs anymore. He wondered if he would always feel hungry for something more.

He slowly and quietly lifted himself from the kitchen chair, slid it back under the table and went to bed.

Chapter 14

Andy and Charlie played ping pong down in the recreation room while they waited for Kathy and Emily to start rehearsals.

Charlie was at the church when Andy arrived. He explained to Andy that he took the city bus because his grandma couldn't bring him. Andy was concerned about the young fellow taking the bus, not alone, having to wait to take the late bus back home at night. He asked Charlie to call home and see if he would be allowed to drive him home. "There's nobody home", Charlie said, "You see my gramma is my foster parent and she has to work all the time. She's not home very much."

The girls made their way downstairs to join Andy and Charlie. Janice was relieved to have a moment to just sit back and watch as Andy took the two young actors through the manger scene.

After running through the script once, Andy joined Janice to watch the kids go through the scene alone. They were both surprised to see just how good the two of them were together.

Janice and Andy talked small talk until Janice asked Andy about his practice. She noticed how good he was with Emily and how much she seemed to like him, so she wondered if he would be willing to take them as new patients. He was pleased to accept them as new patients but warned Janice that the front desk was currently disorganized and chaotic. His office manager just had a family emergency out of state and had to leave without preparation or notice. Everyone one was trying to cover her duties and hours, but admittedly, not with much success.

Janice couldn't hold back her excitement. She shared with Andy that she had been looking for a few weeks now for an office position but seemed to have difficulty because it appeared she had limited work experience since being a stay at home mom. She disclosed to Andy a little bit about her and Emily's situation and he was delighted to offer the opportunity for her to come into the office tomorrow morning, meet the rest of the staff and talk about potential opportunities. She couldn't thank him enough. He was just as thrilled to have the office debacle possibly be ending.

Charlie and Emily finished up practicing for the manger scene and then joined Andy and Janice. The new group of young actors just arrived with Mr. English, the other volunteer rehearsal coach so they gathered their things and exited the church. Andy reminded everybody that they had one more rehearsal next week and auditions were Saturday morning. They said their goodbyes and Andy told Janice he would see her bright and early in the morning.

Janice explained to Emily what Andy meant about meeting tomorrow as she drove back to the shelter. Emily didn't understand why her mom needed a job. She never had a job before. Janice explained that Brad was the one who worked before but now that they weren't at home, Janice needed to make money to pay the bills. Emily asked when they would be going back home. "Honey," Janice reached over and rested her hand on Emily's cheek, "we aren't going back home. We will figure out how you can possibly see your dad, but we will be getting a new home for just the two of us." All the happiness that Janice seen in her beautiful girl's face from earlier drained out. Suddenly Janice wasn't feeling as happy as she had earlier either.

The girls got back to shelter, and Janice got Emily all tucked into bed. Janice went down stairs and met Alicia and Sandy in the kitchen. She told the girls about the job opportunity with Dr. Scutella and they hugged her and offered her congratulations. They reminded her she was courageous and would make it through this painful time. They reminded her this pain was temporary and she will be happy and at peace someday. But, for tonight, they insisted they have a celebratory pastry out of the donations they received earlier. Janice felt much better and more hopeful after her cheese Danish, cold glass of milk, and some words of encouragement from her new friends.

Meanwhile, Charlie and Andy were on their way to Charlie's foster house. Charlie told Andy he was starting to get worried about the upcoming auditions. Andy consoled Charlie telling him some anticipatory anxiety was normal. "But what if I don't get the lead role? What if I can't convince the Hendersons that I'm the boy they should adopt? What if they don't think I'm special enough?" With an ever-growing fondness for Charlie, Andy explained that Charlie didn't have to do anything but be himself. He explained to Charlie that he was special just the way he was, and the right person will adopt him when it's the right time. Charlie looked at Andy out the corner of his eyes. He wanted to believe what he said was true, but he had his doubts.

Charlie noticed a bag of comic books on the floor at his feet. "Cool You like comic books too, Andy?" The rest of the ride to Charlie's house was filled with laughter and banter over which character was the best superhero and who had the best super powers. "You think I like comic books a lot, you haven't met my wife, Linda, yet. As a matter of fact, comic books are what brought us together." Andy remembered as he smiled to himself, both reached for the newest edition of Batman and ended up fighting over it. Andy was so attracted to her bright blue eyes and fiery attitude that he told her he would give up the comic if she promised to have dinner with him. She was smitten with his warm, brown eyes and his comical ways and immediately agreed. They exchanged numbers and later that evening Andy called to arrange their dinner date at the local Italian restaurant. By the end of the week, the two of them were inseparable. Andy shook his head as he thought about how long ago that was and how dire their relationship was at this point. What had become of them? How did it get that bad?

Charlie interrupted Andy's questioning the fate of his marriage by suggesting maybe he could meet Linda sometime. Andy just patted Charlie on his back, "Sure, buddy, maybe you could sometime," hiding his doubt and uncertainty. Just then, Andy realized, he almost drove right past Charlie's street. He found himself wishing he didn't have to drop him off.

Andy gave Charlie one of the comic books and reminded him to rehearse before their meeting next week. After waiting for Charlie to safely get inside his foster home, Andy steered the car toward his own house.

Chapter 15

Andy told Kathy about his conversation with Charlie regarding his desire to meet Linda. "I'm curious why you don't introduce Charlie and Linda", Kathy asked.

"Because I'm afraid she would just feel bothered and not really welcome him."

"Do you know this to be true? Is there any evidence to suggest she would react that way toward Charlie?"

"No, I guess I don't really know."

"Well, it sounds like Charlie is becoming important to you. He sounds like a very nice boy. Maybe Linda would think so too."

"Maybe. I'll ask her if she would meet him."

"Sounds like a plan and a good place for us to leave off for the day."

Andy went home after his appointment with Kathy. He had a free evening and was looking forward to some time for himself. He'd been under so much stress lately.

He pulled into the garage and entered the house through the kitchen. Linda was sitting at the kitchen table, drinking a cup of tea and reading her book. She put the book down and tried to engage Andy in conversation as Kathy had recommended in an earlier meeting.

" Hi. How was your day?", Linda asked, feeling awkward and foolish.

"It was really busy", he said, not even looking at her. He was too preoccupied to notice her or realize she was trying to make a connection with him.

"Anything exciting happen today?'

"Nope. Just busy. I'm going to play a few games and try to relax."

"Oh. Okay." Linda picked her book up again and found the page where she left off.

Andy noticed the chill to her voice and looked at her to see her nose in her book. He thought to himself, "All she cares about are those damn books."

After about half an hour, Andy began to feel hungry and went to the kitchen where Linda continued to read. He asked her if she was going to have anything to eat for dinner. She mumbled, "I already ate." He was frustrated that she never wanted to do anything with him. He didn't know how long it had been since they even ate a meal together. Feeling ongoing resentment and distance, Andy reached in the refrigerator and pulled out the left-over roast and potatoes he cooked over the weekend. He threw the dish into the microwave, poured a glass of tea, and reached into the freezer for some ice. He had to reach around the giant turkey he picked up for Thanksgiving. He loved to cook, and he was looking forward to preparing a whole Thanksgiving feast. He wondered if maybe Charlie would like to come for Thanksgiving. Then he and Linda could meet each other. Forgetting he was feeling angry toward Linda a few seconds ago, the and, now, excited about the possibility of having Charlie for the holiday, Andy asked, "You know, Thanksgiving is almost here. I was thinking about seeing if Charlie could join us. What do you think?"

"Do whatever you want. It seems like you enjoy your time with him much more than you do me anyway."

"What? are you serious? Are you honestly jealous of a little foster kid?"

"Why shouldn't I be? You act like you like him more than me. You talk to him more than me. You laugh and smile and have fun around him. How long has it been since you have done any of that with me?"

"What are you talking about? I'm always trying to talk to you and do things with you. You always have your face in that damn book and you never want to leave this fucking house."

"I tried to talk to you when you came home from work today. You didn't even acknowledge me. You could barely look at me, not alone talk to me."

"Well forgive me for needing a little time to myself. I told you I just needed to relax a little. You know how busy I am. If you even gave a shit, you would understand that."

"If you gave a shit, Andy, you would know I need you to look at me sometimes. I need your attention too. What do I have to do to get you to notice me? To talk to me?"

"Just forget it. I give up!" Andy took the plate, containing the roast and dumped it in the garbage. He sat down at the table across from her, rubbing the back of his neck.

"Andy", Linda said, "we're not doing what we're supposed to be doing. We're supposed to be working on the love languages Kathy taught us. Your supposed to be giving me more positive feedback."

"I know. I try but it's hard to give positive feedback to you when I feel so distant from you. You're supposed to be giving me more affection and physical touch."

"It's hard for me to be affectionate", Linda explained, "when I'm not feeling emotionally close to you."

"Let's try harder, Linda, okay? I want this to work. I want us to work. I'm going to try harder," Andy said with conviction.

"I want us to work too. Come on, let's get out of here. Let's go get ice-cream or something," Linda said.

Andy smiled, got up from the table, grabbed the keys and, together, they walked out to the car to go get their much-earned treat.

The next morning, Linda awoke and got dressed in her favorite purple blouse and went downstairs to greet Andy who was making breakfast.

With as much courage as she could muster, knowing there was a good chance she might get rejected, she reached her arm out with apprehension and rested it on Andy's back. "Good morning. I'm really sorry about last night."

He smiled, knowing how hard she was trying, "Good morning. I'm sorry too. You look very pretty, by the way, that's my favorite shirt on you. It makes your blue eyes just sparkle."

Linda thanked him and rubbed his back. They both sat at the kitchen table over Andy's breakfast of scrambled eggs and sausage. They both felt a little silly and nervous and they both had the biggest, goofiest grins they've worn on their faces in a long time.

Andy and Linda continued to follow through with their homework for the rest of the week and weekend. They were both feeling better, so Andy was hopeful when he asked Linda if she would go to the appointment with him on Tuesday night. Linda agreed and they both delighted in telling Kathy how beneficial the love language homework had been.

During their appointment, Kathy praised them for being courageous by pushing through their discomfort. She urged them to continue and maintain consistency.

By time the couple and Kathy discussed using time-outs and de-escalation during arguments and planning date nights out, it was time to close for the day.

Kathy closed the office after meeting with the Scutella's and drove home. When she got home, she fed Max and herself and then took him for a walk. It didn't take long for her to get too hot and sore from the walk, but she was sure to give herself some positive reinforcement and remind herself she would become more and more comfortable and able to enjoy her strolls with Max the more consistent she was with it. She got herself a large glass of ice water and sat down on the couch with her phone. She had received a message from Sarah, asking Kathy to call her.

"Hi, Mom. What's up?"

"Hi, Kath. You know how Cindy wanted me to go to Washington for a couple of weeks? Well, the only time she is able to have me come is over Thanksgiving."

"Oh. Are you going, then?"

"Well, I want to, but I feel guilty leaving you over Thanksgiving."

"It's okay, Mom. You should go. Will and Amber will be here. We will just have a small Thanksgiving this year."

After talking to Sarah, Kathy then called Will. He answered the phone.

"I've been trying to reach you." Kathy said, "I'm worried about you."

"I'm okay, Kath. I'm just hurting, and I hate my job and I'm just tired. I never have any time off."

"Will you let me know if I can help?"

"I'm okay, Kath."

Kathy told Will that Sarah was going to visit her sister over Thanksgiving. Of course, he had plenty to say about that. They concluded their conversation, agreeing to see each other on Thanksgiving.

"Okay, asswipe. Love you, Kath."

"Love you too, douchebag," Kathy said, knowing her brother wasn't doing well. He hadn't convinced her he was okay, and she was no less worried about him than before the talk.

After talking to Will, Kathy checked her messages. She received a text from Chase. He was quite a persistent fellow.

"I'm finally going to be in your area in the middle of this week for a business obligation and I would love to take you to lunch if you are available. Please don't say no. I need to see you.

Although Kathy was nervous, she was excited to see him too. She had to agree to the lunch date, so she texted him back and the two agreed to meet in the Perkins Restaurant parking lot at 11:30 on Wednesday. They texted a little more back and forth and then Kathy concluded the conversation, wondering what the hell she was going to wear.

The day of the lunch date arrived, and Kathy was ready to get together with her old friend again. She showered and pulled on her typical black pants and flats. Then she decided upon a purple tunic with a golden bar in the middle of the neckline. The purple made her red curls pop and shine. She wore gold, dangling earrings that hung from her ears and rested on her shoulders. It was a sunny day, so she chose a pair of black sunglasses with golden embellishments to top off her look.

She nervously drove to Perkins, keeping her eye open for a large black truck. She could see it in the drive as she was driving toward the lot. Her heart was beating so hard, she felt like she was going to pass out. She tried to take slow, deep breaths to calm down a bit, but she knew her cheeks were crimson in color.

She entered the lot and there he was, leaning against his truck with blue jeans, blue eyes, and dark curly hair.

She instantly smiled, and the anxiety vanished as she jumped out of her vehicle and hurried toward him. He smiled and reached for her, pulling her into his arms. She found herself feeling safe and at home. There was a cozy sense of familiarity. She had been in those arms before and that allowed her to believe she had nothing to worry about.

While still hugging her, he kissed the top of her head and whispered, "It's so good to finally see you, Kathy."

"It's good to see you again, Chase. You haven't changed much over the years," she said smiling up at him.

"You're more beautiful than ever," he said as they began to walk toward the restaurant. "Oops, watch out," he said as he gently pushed her into the bushes lining the walk.

"Seriously? You just couldn't stop yourself, could you?" she asked, pulling herself up.

"You better hurry, woman. I don't have all day," he called back at her, laughing.

He stood, holding the door as she caught up to him. Lunch turned out to be a blast. They joked and laughed and talked about all the funny times they had together many years ago. He didn't quite look at her with those eyes back then. She liked being under his gaze, with his eyes sparkling, and his sheepish grin.

After they were done eating, Chase reached across the table and grabbed her Kathy's hand, "This scares me," he said.

"What scares you?" she asked in return.

"How close I feel to you right now. How right everything feels to be sitting here with you today."

"Oh," she said, not knowing what to say, but adding, "I feel close to you too."

"I feel like I'm falling for you, fast, Kathy."

Just then, the waitress arrived at the table with their check and Chase handed her his charge card. "I have to get back to work soon. Can we try to get together again this week?"

"Sure," Kathy said. "That would be great."

They left the restaurant and headed back to their cars when Chase reached over and grabbed her hand. She was surprised by this gesture but allowed herself to enjoy the feeling of her hand in his.

They walked over to her door, Chase still holding her hand, "I had so much fun," he said to Kathy.

"Me too. Thanks for coming and for lunch."

Chase smiled, leaned into Kathy, and placed his lips lightly upon hers. She startled but before she could pull away, she found herself melting into the comfort of his arms. As they pulled apart, Chase told Kathy he would contact her about getting back together that week and they parted ways.

Kathy's head was swirling with a million thoughts. Things seemed to be moving so fast and that concerned her, but she wasn't really doing anything to slow it down. She was having fun and enjoying herself and it scared the hell out of her. But this was her old best friend. She knew him. She always looked at him as one of the good guys and placed him, somewhat, on a pedestal. Maybe it was ok to take a chance on him.

Thursday came, and Chase contacted Kathy about a Friday night dinner. Friday night dinner turned into him coming home with her and staying for Saturday breakfast. They basked in each other's company and talked about how they felt and if they could see each other in their lives. They both agreed there was something special between them and they were enjoying the path things were going, but they agreed to just take it one day at a time.

Chase left after breakfast and a fast shower. They discussed the potential for another get together soon and, then, they both got back into the swing of their day to day routines.

Chapter 16

It was almost time for Andy and Linda's big date night. He made reservations for the upcoming weekend at the Italian restaurant where they had their first date many years ago. He felt nervous like it was the first date all over again. He started to question, "What if we don't know what to say to each other? What if we end up in another fight? What if we find out we don't have anything to hold onto anymore?"

When the day approached, Andy was overwhelmed at the office. He rushed home, and Linda was already dressed and waiting for him. She wore a bright blue dress and matching earrings that dangled through her lush, blonde hair. Her blue eyes sparkled through smoky hues of shadow swept across her lids. She had been ready for a couple of hours and sat at the table, wondering, "What if he isn't attracted to me anymore? What if he finds me boring?"

She heard his car pull into the garage, so she stood to greet him with a smile, hoping he noticed how much effort she put into preparing herself for the date. Andy rushed through the door and brushed passed Linda. He was stressed and preoccupied and still had to shower and get dressed for the date.

"I'm late", he said, "give me half an hour to shower and get ready."

She lowered her head, disappointed that he hadn't noticed her. As she went to the sink to make a cup of tea, she felt Andy's arms wrap around her waist and he whispered in her ear, "By the way, you look amazing." She turned her neck to look him in the eye and grinned from ear to ear. He winked at her with those eyes of his and she placed a lingering kiss upon his lips before he ran up the stairs.

Linda immediately felt butterflies when Andy came back into the kitchen wearing khaki pants and an emerald green polo shirt. He was clean shaven and ready to go. "All ready?" he asked.

"Yes. I'm starving." He noted to himself that it had been a long time since his wife had an appetite. They used to love to cook and eat together and, one day, Linda just lost her love for food which left Andy feeling even more isolated and alone. It felt good to have this part of her back.

The couple arrived at the restaurant and ordered the works. It was like they had been starving for years. They ordered calamari and salads loaded down with creamy ranch dressing. Andy had juicy clam strips and Linda had golden brown scallops floating in sweet garlic butter for their entrees. They sipped on wine in between bites and conversation. For dessert, the two shared a piece of sky high, silky cheesecake covered in strawberries. As they fought for the final bite, Linda conceded, licking her lips. "I was thinking", she said, "you know Thanksgiving is Thursday. I'd like you to invite Charlie."

"Really?" Andy lowered his fork to the plate.

"Yes. Your dad and my parents are coming. And Kyle and Beth will be here with Kaleb. Kaleb would probably love to have someone here his own age."

"Yes. I think that's a good idea. I'll ask Charlie on Tuesday during our last rehearsal. Thank you, Linda."

Linda reached across the table placing her hand on Andy's and smiled.

"You have no idea how much I've missed that beautiful smile of yours."

The couple enjoyed the rest of their wine and returned home. Both were feeling excited and hopeful for what lie ahead.

That Tuesday night Andy asked Charlie, "Guess who would like to meet you?"

"Who? Linda? Did you tell her I like comic books too?"

"No. I thought you could do that. We want to know if you would like to come to our house for Thanksgiving?"

"Really? Me? For Thanksgiving? Why?"

"Because you're a very special boy and a joy to have around. And I make a mean turkey bird and the best pumpkin pie ever. Plus, my nephew, Kaleb, will be there. You guys are the same age and both like video games and comic books. And, after dinner, we sometimes play a little football if that's something you like."

"Wow. That would be really cool."

Andy had Charlie call his grandma and Andy asked her if he could have Charlie for Thanksgiving. After she agreed, Andy hung up the phone and said, "Looks like you're coming to the Scutella Family Thanksgiving. I'll pick you up about 9:00 in the morning on Thursday.

Andy floated through the rest of the evening, looking forward to telling Linda that Charlie would be coming to dinner.

When he told her, she was both pleased and nervous. Linda didn't have much experience with children. She was the baby of her own family and didn't really have any friends, not alone friends with kids. The one thing she knew was she adored her nephew, Kaleb. But, even though she spent a lot of time with Kaleb, she couldn't stop worrying about Charlie and asking herself, "What if she bored Charlie? What if he didn't like her? How does one talk to an eight-year-old anyhow?"

Thursday morning, Andy got up at dawn and started preparing his stuffing for the turkey. Linda awoke to the sounds of him down in the kitchen, so she got up, went downstairs, and made coffee.

After Andy stuffed the bird and got it in the oven, he and Janet sat around the table enjoying the hot brew. They talked about how glad they both were to be together for the holiday. They acknowledged the work they individually and collectively have done to save the marriage and make it to that point.

After a couple cups, Andy left to pick up Charlie while Linda got dressed and ready for the day. She just made her way back downstairs when Andy arrived home with Charlie by his side.

"Charlie", Andy said, "this is my wife, Linda Scutella."

"Hi Mrs. Scutella. It's nice to meet you." Charlie reached out to shake Linda's hand.

"It's very nice to meet you too, Charlie. Please call me Linda." she reached out and took his hand into her hand. Instantly, a warm feeling flowed through her. She felt elated.

"Andy told me you're a huge comic book fan, even more than he is."

"He did, did he? Well, it just so happens I have collected a few over the years. Come on. I've got something to show you."

She led Charlie down the hallway into a room the couple made into an office/library space. There was a navy-blue couch and two big, fluffy navy-blue chairs. Lamps were on each of the side tables by the couch and two floor lamps with large drum shades hung over the chairs. All along the walls were book shelves with several hundred comic books, along with other books, as well. Charlie's large, round eyes panned the room with awe as he whispered, "Wow. No way."

Laughing aloud and sitting in one of the chairs, she waved her arms around the room and said, "Go ahead. Check them out."

Charlie hustled over to one of the book shelves and plopped on the floor. His sandy hair fell over his eyes as he pulled the books out one at a time.

"I've never seen so many comic books in one place in my life."

"Do you have any comic books of your own, Charlie?"

"I have two of them.", he said with pride, "One from Dr. Scutella. I mean, Andy. and one from my mom before she gave me away."

His voice became small and soft when he mentioned his mother. He lowered his head and played with the pages of the comic he held close to his chest.

"I'm sorry, Charlie. I didn't know."

"It's okay. It was all my fault. I made her mad at me. It was after she had my baby sister. The lady came and took my sister out of the hospital when she was born because my mom was drunk. My mom said, without my baby sister, we weren't going to have much money. I forgot that my mom said we didn't have any money and, when we were in the grocery store, I asked her if she would get it for me. She yelled at me and told me I was a brat. She said I was nothing but trouble. I didn't mean to cry but I did so she ripped it out of my hands and paid for it. When we got home from the store, she called that lady back. The one that took my baby sister. She told her she couldn't handle me or afford to take care of me. That's when that lady came and took me to my Gramma's."

"Oh, Sweetie, I'm so sorry to hear that."

"Do you think it's my fault, Mrs. Scutella? I didn't mean to make her mad at me. I didn't mean to cry. I really didn't."

Linda jumped out of the chair, plopped right down beside the youngster and wrapped her arms tightly around him, feeling his broken heart beating against her own. "No, sweetheart, you didn't do anything wrong." She pulled away, cupping his face and looking into his eyes, "Do you hear me? You didn't do anything wrong." He nodded and sunk back into her chest, wrapping his arms around her. She was surprised by this. Even more surprised was Andy who had just come down the hall to join them and witnessed their exchange. He and Linda caught each other's eyes and smiled at each other. Andy stepped back down the hall and into the living room. He lowered himself onto the couch, his heart full of love for a wife he thought he had lost and a child he just found.

It wasn't but a couple of minutes when Linda and Charlie met Andy in the living room. They plopped down on the couch with him to watch the Thanksgiving parade on television. The aroma of turkey roasting in the oven offered much more to come.

The parade ended, and the house started to fill with guests.

Introductions were made, and everybody welcomed Charlie into the fold of the family. Andy cooked and socialized with his dad who sat at the table watching him. Andy missed his mom, mostly around the holidays. She was a sick woman who made him miserable most of the time, but he loved her. More than he cared to admit. And she loved him even if she didn't know how to show it. She died many years ago from brain cancer. Linda was arguing with her brother, Kyle, about how to set up the new game Kaleb brought so he and Charlie could play. Her parents nibbled on the cheese and crackers that sat on the coffee table, glad to not have to be the ones to figure it out.

Dinner was like nothing Charlie had ever seen in his life. There was a long dining table covered with a giant turkey, stuffing, potatoes, candied yams, macaroni and cheese, coleslaw, rolls, pumpkin pie and apple pie. Everyone was talking and laughing. Silverware was clinking off china and ice was shaken in glasses of tea. Charlie sat high and proud at the table, grinning from ear to ear. So, this is what family sounds like, he thought to himself. Charlie started to think about his friend Jimmy and his parents, Mr. and Mrs.

Henderson. He wondered if it would be just like this when they adopted him, and he became Charlie Henderson.

After dinner and some down time, Andy, Charlie, Kyle, Kaleb, and Beth headed outside to toss around the football. Both Andy's dad and Linda's parents were resting in the living room and Linda started cleaning up. She stood at the kitchen doing dishes and watching the game out the window. It was the first time in a long time she seen Andy so playful and carefree. Everything felt right. It was odd how she watched her husband and Charlie and felt her heart swell. She finished up the plates from dinner and Charlie ran into the house.

"Mrs. Scutella, I mean, Linda, we need another person. Can you come out and play?' Without her typical hesitation and decline, she just dried off her hands and said, "Let's go." The group played and laughed until they were all exhausted. After a short rest over a piece of pumpkin pie piled high with whipped cream, the guests began to head home for the evening.

It was the best day Andy and Linda had in a very long time. In every way possible, they were satiated and full.

Chapter 17

Not everyone had such a joyful Thanksgiving. Janice and Emily were both feeling sorrowful. The whole shelter was abuzz with excitement but neither one of them seemed to be able to get into the holiday. The shelter children were participating in an art therapy group where they cut out and colored various pilgrims and talked about healthy behaviors in families. Emily came to realize, during this discussion about healthy and unhealthy behaviors that her father wasn't healthy at all. She began to see how hurtful her dad had been. Not only to her, but to her mom. She loved her dad, but she could recognize that she didn't feel so stressed and upset since they haven't been around him. She wasn't worried about making mistakes or making her dad angry anymore. Maybe, she thought, Mom did do the right thing by getting them away from him.

All the women participated in some way or another in preparing the large shelter Thanksgiving meal. Alicia was beside herself. She volunteered to oversee the entire production and all the ladies were thrilled to have her in the position. Janice sat at the kitchen table snapping beans. She was quiet and withdrawn. Sandy tried to get her to join the bustle all around her and Alicia cut in and said, "Can't a girl just have some time to think?" She knew Janice was struggling with keeping Emily away from her daddy over the holiday. Janice just wanted the day to be over.

After dinner, which was quite delicious, everyone watched movies in the living area and then headed to their rooms for the evening. Janice and Emily sat up in their room and played cards. Emily shared what she had learned that day in group. Janice just wrapped her arms around Emily and reminded her that it would get better and things would all work out soon. Emily just nodded her head not knowing what "better" would look like.

Janice laid in bed that night thinking about how depressed she was feeling and how she needed to see Kathy as soon as possible. She wondered about Kathy and if she had a nice Thanksgiving today.

Unfortunately, Kathy, had the worst day of them all. She awoke in the morning, determined to move forward with her empowered and independent self and focus on all the joy in her life. She was looking forward to spending some real time with her brother and sister-in-law.

She clicked on the television and watched the news. The newscaster was talking about the Thanksgiving parade getting ready for kick off. She loved the parade and always dreamed of, someday, visiting New York City for the holidays.

She pulled out the roaster and took her turkey out of the refrigerator. After preparing and stuffing the bird, she put it in the oven. She emptied the jellied cranberry into a dish and placed it in the refrigerator to chill. It was Will's favorite and it would never be Thanksgiving without it.

As the morning progressed, and while Kathy watched the parade, she peeled the potatoes and placed them in the crockpot. She candied her yams and made the whipped cream for her homemade pumpkin cheesecake that her whole family loved.

The morning was running smoothly, and Will and Amber would

be there in a few hours. Just as she plopped on the couch to rest a minute, the phone rang. It was Amber who explained Will had been up all night in pain and was miserable. He didn't sleep at all and had taken a lot of medication to try to ease the pain in his back and legs with no success. She stated she didn't sleep well either and felt she was coming down with a cold. They thought it would be best if they just stayed home. Kathy told them it was no problem at all and that she hoped they both felt better soon.

Kathy tried to text Chase. He was having Thanksgiving dinner with his parents, but she so hoped he would be available for a short chat. She just wanted a sense of connection but didn't have any luck getting a hold of him.

Looking down at Max who was sprawled across the couch, Kathy sat at his back paws and said, "You love your momma, don't you Max?" Just then he kicked out his legs, landing a good one in Kathy's stomach. So much for that.

She got up off the couch, basted the turkey, grabbed the cheesecake and a fork and sat back on the couch where she devoured the entire dessert. That concluded Thanksgiving.

Chapter 18

Sarah knew Kathy didn't think it was a good idea to take Will's box of ornaments to him, but she couldn't stand the distance between herself and her first born. He was her baby boy. She loved him more than he would ever know. Being away from him, knowing he was angry with her tore her apart. The mere thought of losing her son threw her into a panic. How could she go on with part of her heart and soul...her very flesh ripped away from her?

She was hoping, if Will looked through the ornaments, it would help him to remember some of the good times they had together and how much she tried to show him she loved him. As a matter of fact, she's done nothing but try to show him how much she loved him. She knew she screwed up and made mistakes and that would haunt her for the rest of her life. She was condemned to a life of guilt and feeling like, whatever she does, it will ever be enough. She spent years being punished for bad decisions. But, dear God, she was so tired. She was breaking under the weight of the pain and guilt she carried. She tried for so long to make amends and fix what was already done. She finally realized she could never fix it. What she needed was forgiveness. She needed her son to accept she was human, and therefore, worthy of love and forgiveness. She prayed someday he would come to understand how she wished things could have been different, how she would fix them if she could and how much she wanted to be loved and accepted by her children.

Will's misery, pain and depression blocked any attempts she made. He just couldn't see past his own hurt. Sarah wouldn't give up on him, though. "Who knows," she thought, "maybe I'm due for a Christmas miracle." With Christmas only a few weeks away, it couldn't be better timing to get Will's ornaments to him. She was sure he and Amber would be putting a tree up soon. Kathy told her they didn't have one up yet, which really isn't like them.

Sarah gently wrapped each of the ornamental memories and placed them safely in Will's box. As she was finishing up her project, the weatherman on the news warned that a winter storm was on its way. He called for heavy snow squalls and below zero temperatures that would progressively increase through the day. Sarah thought to herself that she better get the box to Will in the morning before it started snowing and blowing.

She bundled herself up in her winter coat and boots, grabbed her purse and keys and hugged Will's box to her chest as she closed her apartment door. By time she pulled into the parking lot of the hardware store that Will managed, the roads already had a layer of slush. She parked as close to the door as she could and slipped and slid into the doorway. The box once again held close to her chest.

She stopped the second she seen her son standing in the first isle talking to a customer. To this day, she felt a sense of pride to see the man he had become. She wanted so badly to hug him and tell him how much she loved him and was proud of him but when his eyes met hers, they certainly did not speak to her in a "hug me" kind of way. She could see he was instantly irritated to see her standing there waiting for him. She closed upon herself and adverted her eyes. Maybe Kathy was right. Maybe she shouldn't have come.

Will walked toward Sarah when he was finished with his customer and asked her, "What are you doing?"

"I thought you could use these," she said as she extended her arms to hand Will the box.

"What is that?" He did not take the box from her.

"They are all your ornaments that I have gotten you over the years. "I thought you might like to put them on your tree this year.

"I don't give a damn about any stupid tree. I could care less about Christmas. I just wish it would get over with."

"But what about Amber?"

"I don't know what the hell she's doing. I can't talk about this right now. I'm busy. I got to go." Will turned his back to her and started to walk away.

"Will!" Sarah said his name louder than she intended to. He turned back around to see her standing there holding out that damn box. He grabbed the box out of her hands, mumbled "thanks" and walked away. He was oblivious to her feelings and what she so desperately hoped would come from her loving offer. She could feel her small, round cheeks begin to burn as she walked toward the exit of the store.

"So much for Christmas miracles," she whispered under her breath.

Will took the box back to the lunch room, irritated that Sarah would interrupt him at work for a box of stupid ornaments he had no intention of using. He didn't know why she insisted on bothering him. He was tired and in pain and in no mood to deal with her acting like a big baby.

Chapter 19

Will's day dragged on. Each hour that passed was marked with more pain. His back was killing him, his legs kept buckling under him and he could barely walk. He just wanted to scream. He couldn't take it anymore. He wasn't sure he could keep going on for much longer.

He was sick of dealing with customers complaining and he was sick of his nasty little weasel of a boss.

What was he going to do? The pain was getting worse, he hated his job, his relationship was falling apart, and he was struggling to pay all the bills. There was no way out. He couldn't take any time off. He didn't know what to do to stop all the thoughts. All hope was gone. He pulled out his phone and sent his sister Kathy three words, "I'm so tired."

By time the store was ready to be closed, Will was unraveling. He could barely breathe. He was so distraught and angry. He just couldn't stop thinking. One painful, negative thought after another raced through his head. He felt completely out of control.

He needed fresh air. Once he got outside, he balanced the box Sarah brought under his arm and tried to lock the door. He dropped the damn keys and had to dig through the snow to find them.

After locking the store, he became aware that his truck was buried under about a foot of snow. He automatically grabbed the handle of the passenger side door and felt the sting in his cold, bare fingers as the door resisted being opened. He forgot Amber told him earlier in the week that something was wrong with the door. He went over to the drive's side, threw the box over to the passenger side seat and started the truck.

Rather than taking the time to clean off the vehicle, he turned on the wipers full speed and they slowly moved the heavy, wet snow off the window enough that he could see. He put the truck into gear and exited the parking lot. The snow chaotically and erratically swirled around the truck just as his thoughts were doing in his head.

Will made it to the city limits, all the while, internally preoccupied. He had a 12-mile ride on the open road before he would be safely at home. The roads were covered in a deep layer of snow. The snow was falling so fast and the wind was blowing so hard that the plows couldn't keep up. Will couldn't see more than about a foot in front of him and the headlights of the truck bounced off the falling snow, blinding him in what was otherwise complete darkness.

He was trying to focus on the road, but his brain still wouldn't stop. He struggled to concentrate, and his back was killing him from being so cold and tense. He was aware that he was going faster than he should. His foot was pushing the gas pedal and part of him was saying he better slow down and part of him was thinking he didn't even care. He shook his head as to slow the racing thoughts and finally lifted his foot off the gas pedal. He glanced down at the speedometer to see how fast he was going....52 mph. He looked back up and, in a flash, seen two, wild eyeballs shining in his headlights. He automatically stepped on the brakes and steered away from the deer standing right in front of him.

The truck spun out of control and everything went quiet. The truck did a complete spin and then slid right off the road. Will was in awe at what was happening, and it was happening so damn fast. He was completely out of control. He was very aware at any second the truck could flip over as it was rolling down the steep Centerville hill. He wasn't a praying man but could hear his own voice break the silence as he screamed, "Dear, God, help me!" After the strange voice exited his throat, there was the violent noise of breaking glass and bending metal. Then all was muffled, and silence sat heavily in the air again. Several feet above, the snow quickly covered the tracks left on the road and a deer walked off into the woods.

Chapter 20

Kathy got home earlier than expected, thanks to her last client cancelling her appointment. She noticed earlier in the evening her phone was dead so the first thing she did when she got home was take her phone out of her briefcase and plug it in. She never liked going without an operating phone because she never knew if someone was in a crisis. And the week had certainly been full of them. Kathy found herself barely able to make it through the rest of her work day. Her shoulders felt heavier with each client and she began to panic at the thought that she would not be able to help everybody or meet their expectations. But since she arrived home she was starting to feel some weight lifting, especially knowing she was off for the rest of the week and weekend. She briefly went through her mail and seen a letter from Sam that she received at the office.

She tore open Sam's letter, hoping for good news but what she read was full of mixed messages that left her with an unsettled and ominous feeling. Sam shared that he was doing better since detox but felt depressed and lost. He told Kathy that they put him on new medication and he hadn't felt manic in a while which was the ideal goal...for the staff. It was less than ideal for Sam because he noticed he had anhedonia and all the passion and excitement he felt about his art and his new goals seemed to be slipping away. He was beginning to fear he couldn't be stable and an artist at the same time. He was proud of himself, though, for making the decision to get clean and shared his concerns regarding his moods with the staff so he was hoping they would get it all worked out.

After she read the letter, she buried it deep down into her briefcase. She just needed everything to go away and to relax a little. She took Max outside and, afterwards, fed him. She then stripped down and put on her nightgown, padded around the kitchen in her fuzzy slippers, made herself a hot and steamy cup of tea and a cup of noodles, and cuddled up on the couch. She snuggled up with Max and allowed herself to get taken away from reality by a couple episodes of sitcoms. She finally felt calm and relaxed and headed to bed. She grabbed her phone and took it to the bedroom with her as she crawled into her soft, cozy bed and pulled the blankets up to her ears. She had big plans to bury herself deep into the blankets and wake up whenever she wanted to tomorrow. By time she got all situated, her phone was fully back on and started sounding off that she must have received messages while it was off. Soon as the phone started beeping she could feel herself becoming stressed and panicked again. She wanted to just avoid the messages but knew better.

The first message she opened was from Amber. It just said, "Have you heard from Will?" Well, that was odd for Amber to be messaging her on a week night, especially this late. There were two other messages from Amber and then the next message that came through was Will. The message simply stated, "I'm so tired." The instant Kathy read those three words the blood drained from her face, she gasped and jumped out of bed. Will was in big trouble.

Kathy sent Will the message, "R u OK?" She waited just a couple of minutes, her heart beating loud and fast in her ears. She then called his phone. It rang and rang and then went to his voicemail. "Will, it's Kathy. Are you okay? Please call me as soon as possible." He didn't call. Kathy started running around the house throwing her clothes and shoes on. She grabbed her bag, leashed up Max and headed down to get Sarah. As she was trying to get out the door, she called Amber and told her about the message Will had sent her earlier in the evening. Amber was hysterical. Will should have been home almost two hours ago. What the hell was happening? Why the hell didn't she make sure her phone was charged?

Chapter 21

Will awoke to the taste of blood. He could hear the faint sound of his phone ringing and when he opened his eyes he was looking into the eyes of a storm trooper. At first, he was confused and wasn't sure if he was dreaming or hallucinating. He turned his head to his left to look out of his driver's side window and realized there was no window there. He was, instead, facing the massive trunk of the tree that stopped his truck from rolling and going any further down the hill. He began to remember the accident and the sound of broken glass and bending metal. He looked around the cabin of the truck to assess the damage.

The storm trooper was one of many of the ornaments Sarah had given to Will earlier in the day. They must have been thrown from the box when the truck hit the tree. Besides the ornaments, Will noticed there was shattered glass all throughout the cabin of the truck as well.

As Will observed the glass, it dawned on him how cold he was. He squeezed his fingers and hands together, along with the toes of his feet. He could feel both his hands and his feet so that was good. But they were freezing, and Will realized he was shivering and his lower lip was trembling. He knew he would be in trouble soon with the frigid air infiltrating the cabin of the truck through the open window. It was still snowing, although not as hard as when he went off the road. None the less, it was on him and the interior of the vehicle.

He could still hear his phone ringing. He became hopeful, realizing he could find the phone and call for help. He felt around the seat and reached into his pocket but could not locate the phone. As he pulled his hand out of his pocket he could feel a sharp, burning pain and it felt as if his hand had snagged on his pocket lining. He pulled out his hand to see he had a two-inch shard of glass embedded in the side of his palm. He was shocked to realize he hadn't felt the pain of it before, especially when he was clenching his hands together. He must have been a bit in shock. What else hasn't he realized regarding his dire situations? He began to panic. He still couldn't find the phone and was stuck in the driver's seat with the door blocked by the tree. The passenger side door was already jammed as he realized earlier in the day.

He was feeling colder and started to rub his thighs up and down with his hands. His left hand hit something sharp on his thigh and it sent Will reeling in pain. The pain ran through his body in waves as he began to sweat and feel light headed. He reached up with his right hand and tried to turn the overhead light on. Nothing happened when he clicked it on. "Great! Damn it!" He was in a panic, full of pain and frustrated that he was in this situation. He reached as far as he could and was able to hit the glove compartment button enough for it to pop open. The flashlight and a silver envelope were accessible to him. He turned on the flashlight and expected to see a shard of glass sticking in his left leg. There was glass in his leg, that was true. As a matter of fact, he was coming to realize he had broken glass all along his left side including his head, face, arm, hand and leg. But there was a much bigger problem than that. The source of his excruciating pain was his broken femur bone protruding out of his raw bloody skin and sticking about three inches out of his thigh. Will vomited from the grotesque scene of his mangled leg and passed out.

Chapter 22

Kathy made it to Sarah's apartment in a matter of minutes. The roads were so bad that Kathy knew it was a bad idea to try to make it to Will and Amber's house. So, Kathy and Sarah drove to the police station a few blocks down from Sarah's apartment. They didn't know what to do. The police station had already received a call from Amber and were gathering some information about Will including where he worked, his cell phone number and his typical driving route home.

When Kathy and Sarah arrived at the station, a police officer questioned the ladies about their last contact with Will. Sarah told the officer how upset and aggravated he was earlier in the day and Kathy told them about the message she had received from him sometime in the late afternoon or early evening.

The police officer was comforting to the two women. He was a tall, bulky man in his forties with sandy hair and bright blue eyes that twinkled when he smiled, curving his bright pink lips. He introduced himself as Officer Tommy Phillips.

Officer Phillips got the two women stretched out in a room with a couple of cokes while he left to put an alert out for Will's small red truck.

Kathy, Sarah and Amber continued to stay in contact, checking in via cell phone to see whether either party had any more news or heard from Will yet. All three women were praying Will was just fine and would be located soon.

Officer Phillips finally returned to explain there were several officers looking for Will and soon as anyone heard anything they would be in touch. He told Kathy and Sarah to go ahead home and see if Will tries to contact them. The kind officer gave Kathy his number to contact him if there was any news. The women drove back to Sarah's house trying to comfort one another. Neither one of them disclosed they were petrified he was unsafe.

Kathy couldn't breathe. She kept trying to get air into her throat and down into her lungs, but they felt so heavy and closed off. The one thing she could do was pray and pray she did. "Please, Dear God, bring Will home. Please, Dear God, bring Will home." She repeated those words continuously, determined she wouldn't stop until she knew Will was safe and okay. It was going to be a very long night.

Chapter 23

Will wasn't out long. He knew he had to stay calm and do the best he could to take care of himself. He thought he could try to break out the back window of the truck but knew he would not be able to navigate back up to the road with his broken leg. He then remembered the silver envelope he pulled out with the flashlight earlier. The silver envelope contained a small silver, paper-thin heat blanket. Sarah got it for Will years ago and insisted he put it in his glove compartment. He thought it was ridiculous and worthless but threw it in the box anyway just to placate Sarah. It had been in there for years, never used. He pulled the flimsy silver out of the envelope and covered his body. His phone rang again so he proceeded to look for the damn thing to no avail. He pulled the blanket up to his ears and thought, surely, someone will be looking for him soon.

Will thought about how scared Amber must be since he hadn't come home. He thought about, no matter how miserable he has been and how difficult he was to be around, she loved him. He started thinking about what would happen if he died in that struck.

Would she know how much he loved her? He thought about how short and distracted he was with her. As a matter of fact, the other day she asked him about getting away together and he shot her down fast. He was angry and irritated that she would ask him to travel when he felt so bad. But, as he sat in the truck, he could see her smile fade off her face and her lower her head as she turned and walked away from him. He didn't see it then, but he now realized how stuck on himself he had been. His own pain and misery clouded him from seeing how much he was neglecting the woman he loved.

He thought about Kathy and how much he loved her. She has always been there for him and he knew he hasn't been the best big brother to her. He never checked on her and avoided her calls.

He thought about Sarah as he looked around the cabin of the truck at all the ornaments thrown about. All she wanted to do was let him know she loved him and he pushed her away. He felt ashamed of the way he treated her earlier in the day. Will's eye landed on the storm trooper, still staring at him. He reached out from under the blanket and picked it up off the dash board. He remembered when Sarah got him the ornament. It was the year Star Wars came out in the movie theaters. She took him to the little theater in Titusville which, has since, been torn down. It has been torn down for years, but it used to be a special treat to go. He remembered Sarah was working at the Donut Shoppe, making barely any money but she promised she would take him. She saved money for weeks prior to the movie coming to town. That night they lived it up by going to McDonalds and the movies.

He put the storm trooper down and picked up an ornament that was in the shape of a fish. Both Will and Sarah loved to fish. When he was younger, the whole family would go out fishing in the creek or some of the surrounding lakes. Sara would make sandwiches and pack up a small picnic and they would spend the day out on the water.

Next, Will could see over on the passenger seat, an ornament in the shape of a big, green Oldsmobile. Sarah had written on the front of the ornament the words, "Green Machine". She'd gotten him that ornament the year he received his driver's license. He bought a beat-up Old's and he, Sarah and Kathy would pile up in the Green Machine and drive for miles. He would get lost on dusty, old country roads and was always able to find his way home. They listened to country music like Anne Murray and Alabama and sing at the top of their lungs while laughing at each other. He smiled to himself, thinking about how much fun they had.

Will was still trembling and cold but, son of a gun, the blanket really was helping to protect him from the frigid air.

He spotted an ornament on the console between the two seats. It was dark in the cabin, but the light cast from the white snow all around the vehicle was enough for him to recognize right away which ornament it was. One year, Sarah was into homemade ornaments made of paper Mache and glue. She had taken her favorite picture of Will and herself and attached it on to a heart shape. The picture was of a little, toe headed, two-year-old Will dressed in a tiny blue suit and tie, smiling wide as he sat on the lap of his mommy. Sarah was dressed in a blue plaid dress with her hair styled in a bouffant. She was smiling just as wide. There was no greater picture that captured the love of a proud momma and her baby boy. Will thought about the days before all the anger and hurt and he felt a tremendous sense of grief and loss.

He picked up the last ornament that was within his reach. His fingers open to expose a red heart ornament that had the words, "I will always love you". His fingers squeezed tightly around the promise of love and, for the second time that night, a strange guttural voice exited his throat and he screamed, "Help me!" Then he fell asleep.

Chapter 24

Light began to enter the windows of Sarah's apartment. Neither Kathy or Sarah got any sleep. They were exhausted and horrified as the nightmare of Will's disappearance continued.

There was a knock on the front door and Sarah ran to answer it. Officer Phillips stood in the doorway. Without greeting him, Sarah gasped, "Oh, God. Has there been news about Will?" Officer Phillips looked concerned and stepped into the apartment. Kathy knew it wasn't good news as soon as she seen his eyes.

"I'm here to see if you have a recent picture of Will. There's been an accident involving a red truck and a blue sedan about thirty-five miles from here. We don't know anything yet. It may not even involve Will."

Sarah, crying, asked, "Did they take them to the hospital? Are they okay?"

Office Phillips lowered his head, "No, ma'am, both drivers were killed."

"No!", Kathy pushed the officer away as to push his bad news away. He grabbed her arms and pulled her into him, silently holding her. She pulled away from him and grabbed a framed picture of Will that was setting on Sara's entertainment center.

Sarah and Kathy cried and hugged each other. Officer Phillips hated this part of his job. It was hard, for some reason, seeing these two women break down over the possible loss of their loved one.

Phillips reminded the women that there was no solid evidence that anything has happened to Will and that there were many officers still out looking for him. He stated they were still trying to locate his cell phone and he stated he would be in touch as soon as he knew anything. As he left, he reminded them to have faith.

The snow had stopped, and plows began cleaning the roadways so Amber drove into town to be with Kathy and Sarah. She arrived at Sarah's in time to see the officer who explained the situation to her.

The three women comforted each other, vowing to have faith and hope while they awaited Will's safe return.

Chapter 25

Will awoke again. He was weak, sick to his stomach, and thirsty. He couldn't believe he made it through the night. He knew he was in bad shape and needed help. He could hear vehicles on the road up above, so he knew the plows must be clearing the way. The heavy winds through the night helped to keep the snow from covering the windshield and Will could see a tiny stream of sun poking through the clouds above.

Will could hear the all too familiar sound of a plow truck coming down the road. Its giant blade was dragging along the road, clearing the snow. He thought to himself that a plow truck is high enough that maybe, now that daylight is rapidly breaking through the darkness, that the driver might be able to see his truck down below. It was red which would, hopefully, stick out from the all-white, snowy surroundings.

Jeff Daily, the plow truck driver, was cruising down the road at a pretty good pace. His radio was blaring, and he was using his steering wheel as a make-believe drum set. That's when he seen this one single ray of sun, bright as could be, breaking through the clouds.

Just then, Jeff spotted a deer standing on the opposite side of the road.

"Just stay there. Don't you dare come onto this road you little son of a bitch." Well that was worthless because the deer stared right at him and stepped in the road. Jeff started stepping on the break to slow the big plow down. The deer ran in front of the truck, trotted alongside the road, capturing all of Jeff's attention. The deer headed down the hillside, looked back at Jeff and continued down the hill and, there it was, right in front of the deer and right under the beam of sun...a red truck partially wrapped around a massive tree.

Jeff knew it was dangerous to park the truck on the road, but he pulled off as fast as he could and jumped out on road. He knew he had to see what was going on. He screamed through his cupped hands, "Hello. Hello. Is anyone down there?"

He listened close enough to hear a response, "Yes. Please help me."

Chapter 26

There was a fast wrap on the front door of Sarah's apartment.

Kathy opened the door to see Officer Phillips. His blue eyes met hers

and she knew. Will was okay.

"Come on ladies. Get your things and come with me. I'm taking

you to the hospital. Will has been found and has been transported to

the emergency room. He's in rough shape but he's going to be just

fine."

The women all piled in the police car and couldn't express enough

how elated and grateful they were.

The nurse was getting ready to wheel Will to the operating room.

"Hurry, girls. He's on his way to surgery to fix a badly broken leg."

Kathy was shocked to see her big brother, broken and pale, covered

in wounds and blood.

He didn't say anything, but his wide eyes took in all his girls and his heart soared. Amber gently kissed his right cheek and Kathy looked in his eyes and grabbed his right hand, noticing it was tightly closed around something hard. Sarah found herself apprehensive to run to her son but needed to see him and make sure he was okay. She stood beside Kathy on her right side and met his eyes with hers. He reached his right arm out and gestured for her to give him her hand. She held out her hand, not knowing what to expect. Out of his tightly clenched fist and into her hand fell the red heart ornament with the words, "I will always love you."

"Okay, ladies, off to surgery we go." Will was wheeled down the hall and out of sight.

Chapter 27

Will made it through his surgery and did well. He was being kept for observation and didn't know when he would be released. Everyone was trying to recover from the whole ordeal and find some sense of normalcy again.

Kathy and Chase had become so close that she wanted to share with him everything that had happened with Will. Oddly enough, she hadn't heard from him since their amazing night together at her house. He never returned her text from her attempts to contact him on Thanksgiving. That bothered her, but she figured he may have just gotten too busy with his family and all the holiday gatherings. After that, Will had his accident and chaos took over.

Now that the dust had begun to settle, the first thing she found herself wanting to do was talk to Chase. She sent him a text, realizing for the first time that she couldn't call him because he never gave her his phone number. They only ever communicated through social media messenger.

She was surprised that she hadn't heard from him sooner. He was calling her almost every day, sometimes several times a day. There was a definite change in his behavior. She began to worry about him. Could something have happened to him? Was he okay?

She sent him a message, "Hi. I haven't heard from you. Hope you are okay. Please let me know. I'm worried."

She didn't hear back from him until about 1:30 in the morning when she heard her phone beep, waking her from a restless sleep.

"Sorry. I've been busy. I'm fine. How are you?"

Kathy replied, "I'm doing okay. I've been busy too. There's been a lot going on here that I wanted to tell you about. I've missed hearing from you."

Kathy didn't hear from him again that night. She thought he must have fallen to sleep. She went back to sleep, herself, feeling uneasy.

When Kathy got out of the shower the next morning there was a message from Chase, "Maybe we should just slow down and be friends if my being busy bothers you."

"What?" Kathy thought to herself.

"It doesn't bother me. And I'm not mad. It's just been a while since we've spoken, and I had some things happen that I wanted to share with you. My brother was in a bad accident and Thanksgiving was terrible. I tried to message you on Thanksgiving, but you never responded. Is everything okay?" Kathy felt sick. If a client shared that this was happening to her, Kathy would be having the "he's just not that into you" discussion. She was seeing all the red flags, but it didn't make any sense. Chase just told her before Thanksgiving that he was developing very close feelings for her. They had been getting closer and closer and were spending more time together. The way he looked at her and held her when they were together didn't feel like he wasn't interested or didn't care.

Chase texted back later that day, "I'm sorry. I get this way when I get close to someone. I'm afraid I will get hurt so I push people away. I think we should just be friends for now. Who knows what the future will bring."

Kathy responded, "I thought we were having a good time together and we both said we saw each other in our futures. We agreed to just go slow and enjoy. What changed in a matter of a few days? What's really going on, Chase?"

After a long pause, Chase responded, "I'm sorry. I didn't know how to tell you that I spent Thanksgiving together with my ex-wife and we decided to get back together and give it another try."

Kathy's heart sank. She sat her phone down and cried. She cried rejected and brokenhearted tears and then she cried angry, full of rage tears. And it was a damn good thing he wasn't there, or she would have personally knocked him off the pedestal she had mistakenly put him on so many years ago.

How could he do that to her? How could he encourage her to let her walls down for him, stating she might regret wondering what could have been? How could he tell her she was beautiful and special and that he had thought of her often through the years? How could he tell her he felt so close to her that it scared him? How could he turn around and reject her? How could God have brought him back into her life for this to happen when she was just fine before he came around? How could she be so stupid to think he was any different?

Chapter 28

It was the big night of the play and everyone was excited, except Kathy. She was really looking forward to the play until everything that had just happened with Will and Chase. She wasn't sure she wanted to go but she couldn't let down Janice and Andy. She called her mom who was also recovering from Will's accident and she was thrilled to attend the play with Kathy. Sarah loved the theater. So, they made plans for the evening to go to dinner and then the play.

Kathy did her best to find something to wear that would be nice enough for dinner and a play. She was frustrated with the lack of stylish clothes for someone her size. Most of the things she had were not fitting and hung off her like a garbage bag. And most of the things she wore were black or navy blue. She felt especially frustrated this evening because she was tired and not feeling well. Things have been weighing on her heavily lately.

After settling on a pair of black slacks and black flats and pairing them with a navy-blue tunic and silver and blue earrings, she left to pick up Sarah. Both women were a bit quiet during dinner. They talked about Will and his accident. He was doing well. He was still in the hospital, but Sarah said she thought the doctor might release him this weekend.

Dinner was delicious. After hearty bowls of spaghetti and cheese and the best Italian bread and butter ever, the girls headed to the church. Kathy circled the block a couple of times to find a good parking spot and finally landed a prime spot. They squeezed through the crowd and found a pew that still had some room. She was relieved to know she didn't have to face the daunting question of whether a chair was going to be big enough for her.

After being seated, Kathy started to look around the room. She noticed Andy right away sitting right up front in the first pew and he was beaming with pride. Linda was going to come with Andy to see Charlie, but she ended up with the flu. Although, he was disappointed, he was too excited to see Charlie to let anything bother him.

Kathy continued to look around the room when she heard a familiar voice ask, "May I have this seat?" She looked up to see Officer Phillips standing above her.

"Oh, hi, Officer Phillips. Sure, have a seat," as she slid over, closer to Sarah who also greeted the officer, thanking him again for all his help with Will. He was pleased to hear that Will was coming along and would be able to leave the hospital soon.

"Do you have someone special in the play, Officer Phillip?" Kathy asked?

"Please, call me Tommy. Yes. My nephew is involved with the community art house. They helped build some of the background set, so I promised him I would come and check out his hard work. To be honest, I was dreading it, but now I'm glad I came. How about you?"

"I have a couple of friends that told me about the play", Kathy stated, making sure not to give away the privacy of her clients.

Just then the introductory music began to play, and the lights were lowered. Kathy noticed Janice was sitting in the pew beside the one she was seated in. She was with a couple of other women and they were all smiling and laughing.

A small choir of children in the background started to sing, "Mary, Did You Know?" when two of the play's stars entered the stage. Kathy recognized Emily and Charlie right away by the descriptions she had received over the weeks. Emily was beautiful draped in fabrics, including a long head to toe garment and a veil. Charlie, tall and proud, in his robe, owned that shepherd's staff as he looked out toward the crowd. He squinted through the lights to make sure the Hendersons were there, but he couldn't see well enough. He knew they had to be out there in the crowd. Jimmy promised him, and Jimmy and Charlie had each other's backs. Jimmy wouldn't let him down. Charlie reminded himself that tonight was the night. He had rehearsed for so long and memorized all his lines. He did everything he could and by the end of the night he hoped he would earn a spot at the Henderson dinner table. He had dreamed about having a big, happy family for so long.

The play was a big hit and they were heading into the final scene where Mary and Joseph circle the baby Jesus lying in swaddling clothes. The three wise men stood around and the lights were completed dimmed except for the spot lite shining on baby Jesus. The choir softly sang, "Away in A Manger" as Charlie looked out to the crowd one more time. Since the lights were no longer blinding him, Chase could see Jimmy sitting right in the second pew back. There they were. The Hendersons were smiling up at the stage. Surely, he had captured their attention. When he looked at Jimmy, however, Jimmy looked upset which was a curious thing considering soon they would be brothers. And then he noticed something he had not expected. In Mrs. Henderson's arm lay a small baby boy.

Pain filled Charlie's chest. In one second all his dreams came crashing down. He was distraught and lost. Obviously, he wasn't enough. He tried so hard and it wasn't enough. He was never going to be enough. He looked down at the baby Jesus and one tear slid down Charlie's cheek and landed on the cheek of baby Jesus. How ironic it was that baby Jesus looked like he was crying too.

The music ended, and Charlie ran off the stage, ripping off his robe before he even exited off the side. All the other children began to exit the stage as well.

Andy knew right away something was wrong. The boy he was growing to know and understand just collapsed upon himself right in front of Andy's eyes. Andy got up and ran to the back of the stage to find Charlie. Just as he came around the back of the stage, Charlie was running down the stairs leading off the stage. Andy reached out to him, "Charlie? Are you okay? What's happened?"

"Get away from me!" Charlie screamed at Andy. Andy was startled by Charlie's response and took a step back, still holding his arms out, empty. The back stage was filling up with children and parents, all hugging and celebrating their children's success.

"This is your fault! You made me think I could be loved. You made me think I was good enough to get adopted. But you lied! The Hendersons don't want me. They never wanted me. Nobody wants me! Just leave me alone!"

"But Charlie..., " Andy tried to stop him.

"Leave. Me. Alone." Charlie seethed and turned his back to Andy.

Andy went over to Pastor Dom who promised to go right away to Charlie and try to help him. He promised he would, personally, make sure the boy got home safely.

After ensuring the heartbroken boy would be taken care of, Andy walked toward the back door leading to the outside. He looked at the happy crowd one last time and then pushed his way through the heavy metal door. It slammed shut behind him, closing out all the light, and leaving him standing in complete darkness. All the singing and laughing was gone and he was enveloped in silence.

Andy drove home after leaving the church. He was crushed by what had just happened with Charlie. The last few weeks with the youngster had been the best few weeks he had in a long time. Now, he could feel all those feelings creeping back in. He felt empty and worthless. What had he done? How could he screw up so badly to make Charlie so upset? He pulled his car into the garage and entered the cold, dark house. There were no lights on, no "hello", no warm embrace and no one to comfort him or share his feelings with. Linda was already in bed sleeping. He looked at the clock on the kitchen wall. It was only 8:20 pm. He shook his head, opened the refrigerator and looked for something to eat. Maybe he would feel better once his tummy was full. He made himself a ham and cheese sandwich and then ate the leftover spaghetti from yesterday. After the spaghetti, he polished off the last two slices of apple pie. He only felt worse.

He found his way upstairs to his and Linda's bedroom where he crawled into the bed beside his wife. This time, however, she called his name and turned on the light switch. She looked into his eyes and knew things didn't turn out well. "I'm sorry", she said and snuggled in close beside him as she wrapped her arms around him.

Chapter 28

The play had taken a bad turn for Janice too. Just about the time,

the choir was singing "Away in A Manger, the hair on the back of

her neck stood up, warning her something was not right. She hadn't

felt like that since she was with Brad. Brad? She turned her neck

slowly and glanced behind her when her breath caught in her throat

and she gasped for air. She began to tremble and, Sandy recognizing

this, grabbed Janice's arm.

"What's wrong?" she whispered to Janice, "You look like you just

saw a ghost."

"More like a monster," Janice said. "He's here. Brad is here. He's

standing in the back."

Janice sat there wondering what she should do. The choir ended,

the lights came on and the children began to exit off the stage.

Finally, she decided to have Sandy and Missy go to the back of the

stage and get Emily and get her safely onto the van. She walked to

the back of the church where Brad was standing.

"Hey, baby, I'm here to take you and Emily home. Where is she?" Brad reached out to grab Janice's hand. She yanked her hand back as her skin began to crawl beneath his touch.

"You leave her alone. You're not supposed to be here. How did you know we were here?"

"Emily called me," Brad said, shrugging his shoulders.

"What?" Janice couldn't believe Emily called him. She couldn't have possibly, could she?

Brad's brows began to furrow, "What the hell are you waiting for Janice? Emily called me. She wants to come home with me. Now go get her."

"No," she said. "She isn't going anywhere with you and neither am I. You're violating the PFA. You need to get out of here."

"I'm not going anywhere without my daughter. You can't keep me away from my daughter. Come on," Brad grabbed her arm and pulled her out the front door and down a hall to the left that led to the Sunday School room.

"Leave me alone. Let me go." Janice tried to pull out of his grip. Almost everybody was in the back of the church and exiting out of the side doors that led to the parking lot. It was dark and quiet where Brad and Janice were. Brad twisted Janice's arm and slammed her back against the wall. She heard her arm crack and she gasped in pain. She knew she was in trouble. No one could hear her and there was a good chance that Brad could kill her right in the church. She tried to scream, "Help me!" She fought to get away from him as he struggled to cover her mouth with his dirty hand.

"No one's going to help you, you bitch. They wouldn't if they could. You're a piece a shit."

"Step back. Right now. Raise your hands and step back." Brad turned around to see a large police officer pointing a gun at him. Officer Phillips who thought something didn't look right about Brad, excused himself as Kathy and Sarah left the play, so he could keep an eye on him. When he slipped out of sight, Phillips went looking for him. He grabbed Brad's wrists and handcuffed him while reading him his rights. Brad pleaded with the officer.

"Officer, you don't understand. This woman kidnapped my daughter and is trying to keep her from me. This is all her fault. I was working hard for my family and she up and left, taking my kid."

Officer Phillips asked Janice about what happened, and Janice pulled her PFA papers out of her purse and showed them to the officer. He called for support and a patrol car then escorted Brad out of the church. Officer Phillips had also called for an ambulance to check on Janice.

By time the ambulance arrived, everyone was gone except the shelter van with Sandy, Jill, Melissa, Jeff, Emily and Linda, the driver. Sandy came back into the church looking for Janice and found her it the church entrance with the EMT's. They were going to take her to the hospital to get a cast on her arm. Sandy and Janice decided it was best for everyone to return to the shelter without Janice and, once she was all fixed up, Sandy would go to the hospital and pick her up.

"Please don't tell Emily about what happened with her dad. All she needs to know is I fell into the wall. Let Emily know I'll be home soon."

Chapter 29

Charlie, having the worst night of all, was broken hearted and just as distraught as his rehearsal coach. All his dreams came crashing down around him that night. He just wanted to curl up and die.

After he pushed Andy away, Charlie ran down to the recreation room where they rehearsed weeks prior to the production. It was dark, except for the light that came from the hallway. He hugged his knees to his chest and sobbed.

"Charlie?" Pastor Dom called as he peeked into the dark space. Charlie didn't answer him. He just wanted to be left alone.

Pastor Dom reached into the room and turned the light switch on at the wall. He pulled up a chair next to Charlie and sat quietly beside him.

"How did you know I was in here?" Charlie asked.

"Someone who cares very much for you told me you might be in here and asked me to check in on you."

"Who? Andy?"

"Sounds like you were pretty hurt and disappointed tonight," Pastor Dom said as he nodded his head to Charlie's question.

Feeling embarrassed that he thought the Hendersons would really want to adopt him, Charlie brushed off the pastor, "I don't want to talk about it."

"I understand," Pastor Dom said, "If you ever do want to talk about it, I'll be right here. But I can tell you one thing. You are a child of God, Charlie. And He loves you very much and He made you to be a very special young fellow. And, even though things didn't work out the way you wanted them to tonight, He has a much greater plan for you."

Charlie looked up at the pastor, "Do you really think He loves me?"

"I know He does, Charlie," he said, "Now, come on, let me give you a ride home."

As the two walked out to the car, Pastor Dom said, "You were brilliant tonight, Charlie. You did such a good job of learning all your lines. I'm proud of you and all your hard work."

"It didn't really feel like work." Charlie said. "I had a lot of fun spending time with Andy."

"He sure was worried about you tonight. He cares very much for you."

Charlie lowered his head, "I'm mad at him."

"Oh?" Pastor Dom asked.

"He told me I was going to be adopted. He told me I was good enough."

"Well, I believe those things too, Charlie. Are you angry with me?"

"No", he said with confusion.

"Hmmm. I wonder if you were really mad at Andy or if you were mad and hurt that the Hendersons adopted another child."

"I guess the Hendersons," Charlie said, understanding Pastor

Dom's point.

Pastor Dom pulled up to Charlie's house and Charlie slid out of the car and thanked him for the ride. "Oh, Charlie, could you come to the church tomorrow night and help us clean up and put the set away?" Charlie agreed then waved goodbye as he turned to go inside.

Charlie curled up on the sofa bed in his grandma's living room and considered what Pastor Dom said. He picked up the Batman comic book Andy had given him and thought about all the fun he had with Andy and Linda and their family. That's the only time he felt wanted and like he fit in somewhere. He felt like he had a big, happy family when he was with them. That's what he's been wanting all along. And, now he ruined it. He pushed Andy away and told him to leave him alone. What if he never seen him again? What if he ruined his chance to be loved for good?

Chapter 30

Andy awoke the morning after the play and instantly wondered about Charlie. He wanted to call him and see how he was doing but Charlie told him to leave him alone. Maybe he should.

Andy's work day dragged on forever and he continued to be preoccupied with thoughts of Charlie and whether he was okay. He knew he had gotten home safe because Pastor Dom had been kind enough to call Andy and let him know he drove Charlie home. While the pastor had Andy on the phone, he asked him if he would be able to stop by the church that night to help with tearing the set down and putting everything away so that the stage was cleared for the additional Christmas trees they displayed during the Christmas season. There was already one decorated and on display for the play, but they usually flanked both sides of the stage with two trees each. Pastor Dom made sure to let Andy know that he had asked Charlie to help that night as well.

Andy called Linda about going to the church after work. She wished him luck and told him she'd wait up for him to see how it went. He thanked his wife, feeling closer to her than ever. Just before he hung up, he pulled the phone back to his ear. "Linda," he said.

"Yes?"

"I love you", he told his wife.

"I love you too, Andy."

Andy managed to get through the rest of the work day. He grabbed a bite to eat and then headed to the church. He didn't know what to expect if he saw Charlie. What if he was upset to see him? What if he was still mad?

He got into the church and headed toward the stage when he heard Charlie's excited voice say, "Andy", as he jumped off the stage and ran to Andy, impulsively wrapping his arms around him. Andy, surprised by Charlie's reaction, hugged him back.

"Charlie, I'm so glad you're here. I'm so sorry about last night."

"I was afraid I would never see you again," Charlie said, " I'm sorry I got mad."

"You don't ever have to feel bad for getting mad and you don't have to ever worry about not seeing me."

"Okay", Charlie said.

"I want you to know I will always be here if you need me, Charlie. Okay?"

"Okay," Charlie said, nodding his head and grinning from ear to ear.

"Okay. Now let's get this set torn down."

It didn't go unnoticed by Andy that he and Charlie were the only ones there to take down the set. He smiled and reminded himself to thank Pastor Dom later.

After getting everything down and put away, Andy took Charlie for ice-cream and then drove him back to his foster home.

Linda stayed true to her word. When Andy floated into the kitchen, she was sitting at the table waiting for him. She was thrilled that it worked out and shared with Andy her own desire to spend more time with Charlie.

"Really?" Andy was surprised."

"He's a very special boy", she said, "something feels right when he's around."

Andy reached for her hand and cupped it in his own. "I feel the same way. Like..." At the same time, both said, "It's meant to be."

It was Linda the next day, who asked Andy about inviting Charlie over for the weekend.

There were only three weeks until Christmas and the weatherman called for snow. Andy noticed how animated his wife was in discussing spending time with Charlie. She had her spark back and this thrilled and excited him to no end.

The two agreed to see if Kyle, Beth, and Kaleb could meet tomorrow for sledding in the park and then, later that day, the Scutella's and Charlie could go Christmas tree shopping.

Andy called Charlie with the invitation and he was excited. "Can

I come tonight?" he asked.

"You want to come tonight?" Andy asked as he looked over to Linda, she nodded her head with a big smile on her face.

"Linda and I would love that. I'm on my way now."

Andy and Linda pulled up in front of Charlie's house. It had seen better days and was in significant disrepair. The paint was pulling off the front of the house and several pieces of the banister were broken. Charlie was standing on the porch waiting. He ran over to the car and jumped in the back seat.

Hi there, buddy. Are you hungry? We thought we could go have pizza and rent a movie."

"I'm starving," Charlie said as his mouth watered from the thought of eating pizza, a rare treat, never eaten at home.

The three of them huddled over an extra-large pie with cheese and pepperoni, gobbling bites while laughing and talking about the upcoming weekend.

Charlie shared with the couple that he had never participated in picking a tree before. He told them his parents and his grandma couldn't really afford a tree, not a real tree anyway. His mom never had a tree, but his grandma has a little fake one she pulls out and sets on the table every year.

"What do you think you look forward to the most this weekend?" Andy asked.

"Being with you guys," Charlie said.

After a full belly and about half of the movie, Charlie was deep asleep on the couch. The Scutella's shut off the flick and headed up to bed themselves. The next day promised to be full of adventure.

The following day was the best day of Charlie's life and the best day Andy and Linda had in a long time.

Charlie awoke to the smell of sausage, scrambled eggs, and toast. He padded into the kitchen where Andy was manning the frying pan and Linda was operating the toaster. They were whispering and laughing, trying not to wake the young fellow.

They all greeted each other, and Andy poured Charlie a glass of milk and coffee for Linda and himself. The couple teased Charlie for finally waking up after snoring all morning. The three of them filled up on breakfast. After they had plenty to eat, Linda went to get dressed and find enough gloves, scarves, and hats for everyone while Andy put the ingredients for chili together in the crockpot for when they got home later that day. Afterwards, they huddled in the car, Charlie barely able to move with all the additional pieces Linda put on him, and headed to the park to meet Andy and Linda's family.

Sledding was a blast. Charlie and Kaleb competed in how long they could ride the hills before falling off. Then it was all out war when the Scutella's and Charlie bet the Bennetts they could go the furthest.

Unfortunately, after a big sled rollover, the Scutellas had to hear for the rest of the morning how much the Bennetts rule.

Everyone started getting cold and tired, so they huddled over thermoses full of hot cocoa and then went their separate ways.

After warming up and refueling, the Scutellas and Charlie went off to go Christmas tree shopping. Eventually, the three of them selected a six-foot Blue Spruce that the attendant wrapped and helped them secure to the top of the car.

They kept the Christmas tradition overload going as they drove home to "Over the River and Through the Woods" playing on the radio. By time they arrived home, the group was starving so Andy and Charlie put the tree in the stand while Linda served up Andy's chili in big, ceramic bowls.

After eating, they spent the evening decorating the tree. It was an amazing day. Everything felt right. Andy and Linda felt closer and closer to each other. They knew they still had work to do but they felt they finally knew what caused the problems between them and what they needed to do. Charlie had never been so happy. It was the first time he felt like he could just be a kid and was safe and protected. He felt loved. Everything felt right for all three of them. But was it too good to be true?

Chapter 31

Kathy was struggling the week after the play. Christmas was getting closer and closer and it seemed like everything was spiraling out of control. Will was still in the hospital and Kathy couldn't stop thinking the accident was her fault. She still chastised herself for not keeping her phone charged and on. She felt traumatized by the entire ordeal and wasn't rebounding like she thought she should. Some of her clients weren't doing well with the holiday season upon them and depression was prevalent. She still felt foolish and embarrassed for falling for Chase, and although she knew she had to discontinue talking to him, she missed feeling wanted and cared for, even if it wasn't true or genuine.

She dragged through the week, not feeling herself and certainly not on her game. She finally made it through to Wednesday and only had one more work day to get through. She had Friday and the weekend off and planned to lay low.

She was just finishing up her day when she heard the lobby door open. It was Barb Steinman, Sam, the artist's mother. She recognized Mrs. Steinman right away since she had driven Sam to his appointments many times. She looked worn and lost with her hair hanging limp at her shoulders. She wore navy blue sweatpants and a gray sweatshirt with no coat.

"Oh, hello, Mrs. Steinman. How are you? Sam's not here today."

"I haven't been well, Kathy. I'm sorry. I guess you don't know about Sam."

Kathy felt the blood drain from her face and panic race through her body for the second time in a couple of weeks. "What's wrong? What happened?'

Barb lowered her head, her fine hair fell over her eyes, "Sam overdosed last week on heroine. We buried him last weekend."

Kathy was distraught, "What? Oh, no! What happened? I thought he was doing okay."

"He was. He was working his treatment program and just found out about a week ago that he got approval to teach an introduction to oil painting class at the college."

"I know he was having a hard time adjusting to stability and not having his manic episodes," Kathy said, trying to make sense of Sam's death.

"I think he just couldn't find the balance he needed to be passionate and alive and, yet, stabilized and functional. And those damn drugs and alcohol just wouldn't let him go...no matter how hard he tried," Barb muttered as she lowered her head to hide her tears.

"Anyway," she said, forcing herself to hold back her pain, "I went up to his room for the first time since he died, and this was sitting by his desk. I wanted to make sure you got it. Thank you for trying to help him Kathy. I know everybody tried to help him. He just couldn't help himself. I guess he was beyond help." She turned and walked out of the door, leaving Kathy holding what felt like a canvas wrapped in brown paper with her name written on it. Kathy lowered her body down into a lobby chair and slowly traced the letters in her name written in his handwriting.

She slowly peeled the paper from the canvas as to not destroy it. The canvas was an oil painting in ethereal like colors and lines. There were swirls of watery blues and greens and purples, the same colors on his hands and fingernails from the day they last met, the piece he had painted all night before coming to see her. On the bottom of the canvas was a verse,

"I'll call the unloved and make them beloved".

Kathy turned the canvas over to see he had scratched something in dark ink on the wooden frame. "Thank you for helping me to see that, no matter how broken I feel, it's not too late to be someone important. It's not too late to love and be loved."

Her heart broke. It was too late. She couldn't help him to stop using long enough to see those words come to fruition. He was dead.

That was it. Kathy became numb. There was nothing left. She had nothing left. She grabbed her briefcase, the canvas, and her coat and walked out the door. She crawled into her SUV and started it up. She, somehow, ended up at her front door and let herself in. She patted Max on the head, mumbled, "Hi Pumpkin." and fed him his supper. She let Max out after he ate, called him in, gave him a biscuit and curled up on the couch.

After Max finished his biscuit, he tried to pull Kathy up by repeatedly placing her hand in his mouth and backing up. She wouldn't budge. She couldn't move. Eventually, Max gave up trying and jumped up on the couch, curling up behind her knees.

She awoke about an hour later when she heard Max barking out the front window. She went to her bedroom, got on her nightgown and crawled under the blankets.

Max soon joined her, snuggling up to her side.

Kathy tossed and turned throughout the night. In the morning she made tea, contacted all her clients and cancelled their appointments. She, then, left a message for her mom that she didn't feel well and would be home for the day, took care of Max, and then crawled back into bed again.

Kathy felt broken. She spent the afternoon under the blankets trying to mend herself and sooth her own soul. She knew how to get back on her own feet but everything she used to do to get her shit together wasn't working. There had been so much accrued stress that her typical coping strategies just weren't cutting it. It felt like the world was crashing down around her and, no matter what she did, it just kept crumbling down. She felt the burden of death, addiction, painful childhoods, broken hearts, self-blame, and guilt. She was smothering under the weight of it all.

All she could do was try to breath slowly and rhythmically and, eventually, she fell deep asleep. During the night, Kathy dreamt catastrophic, anxiety-driven dreams. She dreamt she was being chased and, no matter how hard she tried, she couldn't get away from this being, looming over her shoulder. Most would think that when she turned around she would have seen some sort of grizzly, gruesome monster, or some serial killer chasing her down with a ragged blade. But, none of those horrible creatures were behind her. In her dream, she would try to turn around fast enough to see what she was running from but each time she turned around she couldn't see the being. So, she ran to a giant antique mirror to see what was behind her and all she could see was herself. That was it. It was herself that she was running from. She realized she was personalizing and owning problems that didn't belong to her. She became aware that she had spent her whole life unrealistically filtering out evidence to support her belief that she was responsible for others and that she failed and disappointed them all the time. That was classic child of an alcoholic thinking. She had determined she must be unlovable and unworthy because no one seemed to worry about her or care about what she was going through. No one ever chose her. Her dad chose alcohol, her mom chose to leave, her brother chose to be internally preoccupied, her best friend didn't choose her, the boys didn't choose her. She realized she had been personally burdening herself for a very long time to prove she was worthy enough and it was all bullshit. She knew, now, she had to let everybody be responsible for themselves and their own choices and behaviors. She also knew she had to be responsible for herself and she had to care for herself the way she wished others would have. She had to choose herself.

When Kathy awoke the following morning, she knew she had gotten the answer to what she needed to do. The weight on her shoulders and the inability to breathe started to slowly melt away. She knew she needed to appreciate herself, to have more kind and realistic expectations for herself and to offer herself forgiveness, support, and encouragement. She decided to give herself the love she waited so long to receive from others. That's where it needed to be most of all, within herself.

She threw her blankets off and jumped in the shower. She imagined the pain, guilt, and shame running off her body, slowly rolling down her curves and right down the drain.

Kathy dried her long hair, got dressed and sang, "Come on Max. Want to take a ride?" Max pranced around her with excitement as she grabbed her purse and leashed him up. She knew what she had to do so she drove to the store and bought two things. The first thing was a tiny, little Christmas tree decorated in bows and bulbs and, the second thing she bought was a bag of chocolate covered vanilla cremes.

She drove through the iron gate and drove down the small road until she was sitting beside her father's grave again. She peered out the side of her window and then opened the candy cremes, taking just one piece and putting it in her coat pocket. She grabbed the tiny tree and told Max, "I'll be right back, Pumpkin. Be a good boy. I have to have a quick talk with Dad."

Kathy walked through the snow and felt around the snow-covered ground to locate and wipe off her dad's plaque etched with the words "George Roth". She sat the tree down on the plaque and called, "Dad?" She stood there in silence, once again, losing her words, not knowing what to say. But she urged herself confidently to not give up and turn away again. So, she just started rambling, "Dad, do you remember the last time we saw each other? Well, I do. I haven't been able to get it out of my head since I found out you were dead. I've never told anybody this, Dad, but I must get it off my chest. I need to forgive myself and you too. It was New Year's Eve. I hadn't heard from you since before Thanksgiving and we didn't talk at all for Christmas. I knew you were drinking heavily again. On New Year's Eve, I was driving down the street and ahead of me, I recognized your small frame and your typical jacket and jeans. You were carrying your big art attaché case that was almost as big as you. I knew you were probably finding buyers who, while taking advantage of you being drunk, would give you a few dollars for artwork that should have been sold for hundreds of dollars so that you could buy yourself more beer for the night. I got up to beside you, Dad, and the light turned red. You were waiting to cross the street, stumbling and tripping over yourself. I watched you, with your face flax, your mouth hanging open and your right eye that was always half closed when you were wasted was, indeed, half closed. You looked at me and I looked at you. I despised what I seen in you, Dad. I was so angry at you for always making me feel like I had to make you better or fix you. I stared at you with resentment for always leaving me full of guilt and shame. I don't know if you even realized you were looking at your daughter. The light turned green and I drove off, right passed you. A voice in my head told me that would be the last time I ever saw you alive and I just kept driving. I'm so, so sorry, Dad. I love you so very much, but I just couldn't try to save you again. I get it now, Dad. Those were expectations I put on myself. I now understand and accept that was the first step in me learning to self-preserve. I needed to save myself. I no longer feel guilt or self-blame for that choice. I had to realize I couldn't save you. I tried for

215

too many years. You needed to save yourself, Dad. And you didn't. You failed yourself and you failed me. You just couldn't break free from the hold the fucking alcohol had on you. But I forgive you and I love you because I know you tried sometimes, Dad. You tried."

Kathy took a deep breath bringing cool air into her lungs. She could breathe a little easier.

"Bye for now, Dad. I love you and I miss you. Oh, yeah," she reached in her pocket and pulled out the candy creme. "I brought you your favorite." She placed the candy on the plaque by the tiny tree and whispered, "Merry Christmas, Dad," and slowly walked through the snow back to her car.

Chapter 32

Janice got out of work late. She had just enough time to cash her check and stop by McElroy's to pick up her Christmas layaway. She was excited to show Alicia what she bought Emily for Christmas. She was proud of herself for being able to get Emily some gifts after everything they have been through and she wanted to tell Alicia that she was right when she said everything would work out. With hard work, support, faith and a little prayer, she and Emily were going to be okay.

She picked up Emily and headed back through the snow and toward the shelter. They stepped into the warmth of the shelter and it wrapped them in its embrace, pulling them in from the cold. Emily went to hang out with Jill and Janice put her things away and headed to the kitchen. She and Alicia had dinner duty tonight for the shelter and Alicia was going to teach her how to make her old family five bean dinner recipe.

She waited about half an hour for Alicia, but she didn't show up. She looked all over the shelter and asked everybody if anyone had seen her and nobody knew where she was. The staff told Janice to go ahead and start dinner without her since it was getting late. She prepared fish sticks, french fries and green beans. The whole time she was thinking it wasn't like Alicia to be late for house chores, especially cooking. Alicia loved to cook and share recipes with the other women.

Janice became worried as the evening progressed. Curfew was at 8:00 p.m. and it was already 7:30. She called Alicia's cell phone throughout the evening, but it just rang several times before going to voicemail. Her instincts were telling her something was very wrong. She and Emily and some of the other residents watched Rudolf The Red Nose Reindeer and then Janice got Emily up to bed. She pulled out her phone again and called Alicia with no luck.

Janice finally went to bed herself and tossed and turned all night with worry. She must have finally fallen asleep because she awoke at 8:00 a.m. to the sound of coffee brewing. She jumped out of bed, threw on her robe, and went downstairs. She quickly walked through the living room where Emily and Jill were watching cartoons. Alicia was always up early, sitting in the kitchen with coffee and doing the puzzles in the paper. She was disappointed to see the kitchen was empty and the newspaper was still rolled up on the table. She ran back up the stairs and knocked on Alicia's door but there was no answer. She peeked in, but Alicia wasn't there. Panic gripped her chest, stealing her breath away. She knew something was wrong. She ran to the office and asked if they heard form Alicia yet.

"Janice, come in and sit down," Pattie said.

"Janice, we're worried about her too, but women decide to leave the shelter all the time without telling us. We need to consider the possibility that Alicia decided to go back home. If that is the case, we will pray for her safety and we will be here if she decides to come back."

Janice nodded and got up. She just couldn't believe Alicia would go back, especially after everything she shared with Janice. But she hadn't known Alicia for long and she did hear her talking to Calvin on the phone that one night. Janice just thought Alicia would tell her if she was going to go home. She would tell her "goodbye". She kept remembering Alicia saying, "I've been in this shelter six times. There won't be a seventh." Shaking her head, Janice went to the kitchen to do her chores, feeling heartbroken, nervous and alone. She needed her friend.

It was quiet all day in the shelter. Everyone got news that Alicia didn't return to shelter and many of the women were convinced she must have returned to her abuser.

By time the six o'clock news was over, everyone in the shelter would know why Alicia didn't return to the shelter. The anchorman on Channel 35 stated a male and female were found dead in their home when police arrived after neighbors heard gun shots. It was determined the man, Calvin Dillinger shot and killed his wife, Alicia Dillinger, in a domestic dispute, before turning the gun on himself.

Janice was devastated. Alicia was right. She would never return to shelter for the seventh time.

There were no services for Alicia after her death. In a small will and testament, Alicia requested that there not be any services because she was afraid no one would come. She thought no one cared enough for her to be there. She didn't have any children. Her parents were deceased long ago. But she didn't realize just how important she was to people, especially Janice. Alicia kept her sane and grounded through this whole ordeal. She helped her to stay safe. And she would never be forgotten.

Janice sat by the Christmas tree in the dark that night after finding out what happened to Alicia. Everyone was in bed, but she couldn't rest. She thought about Alicia as she held the ornament she had given her in her hand. She turned the sparkling heart around to see the words, "You are loved." She pulled out her phone, dialed an old and familiar phone number. All she could mutter was, "Mom?"

A loving voice on the other end simply said, "Come home, honey."

The following day, Janice had an emergency appointment with Kathy. Kathy listened as Janice told her about Alicia's death. Her heart broke for both Alicia and Janice. The two women talked about grief and then Janice told Kathy she decided to go home to see her parents in Florida over Christmas and didn't plan on returning to Pennsylvania.

Although Kathy was sad to see Janice leave, she knew she had come a long way and would benefit from the support of her loved ones. She was ready to make a new life for herself and Emily.

After saying a difficult goodbye to her therapist, Janice then called Dr. Scutella to thank him for the job and to say goodbye. He gave her a chance to see that she could re-enter the work force and support herself and her daughter. He also promised to give her a good referral as needed.

Janice did the best she could with her broken arm to pack her and Emily's things. All the shelter residents and staff helped her to load her SUV and, after hugs and goodbyes, Janice and Emily piled up into the vehicle. They were on their way to their first family Christmas in many years. Janice reached in her coat pocket and pulled out Alicia's ornament. She strung the heart from the rearview mirror and pulled away from the shelter for the last time.

Chapter 33

Andy and Linda were starting to enjoy their time together again and were starting to see a future for themselves again. They both felt they had their friend, their spouse, their supporter back. Additionally, they were feeling happier and healthier as individuals. Andy was taking better care of himself and trying to find more balance in his life and Linda had become more inspired and started to write a little in an old notebook she had tucked away in her bed stand a long time ago.

One day, the two of them were talking about going to Comic-con and Linda said, "I bet Charlie would love to go."

Laughing, Andy said, "Ironically enough, I just thought the exact same thing."

"I think about him a lot", Linda said, "I sometimes think how wonderful it would be if we could get him out of his foster home and provide him with something more stable."

"Really? Andy asked. "I think about that all the time. You mean like adopt him?"

Linda shrugged her shoulders, "Why not? He's such a joy to have around and it gets harder and harder to take him home."

Andy smiled and reached over placing her hand in his. She smiled back like they were plotting the greatest adventure there ever was and they both laughed aloud at their brilliant idea.

Christmas was getting closer every day and Andy and Linda found themselves wanting to spend more time with Charlie. They both were hoping he could spend some time with them over the Christmas holiday, so Andy gave him a call to offer an invitation. Charlie had been hoping he would be able to see them again soon and was glad Andy called. Charlie told Andy that he wanted to come over, so Andy asked to speak with his grandma. The scratchy, rough voice of the older woman came onto to the phone.

"Hello ma'am. This is Andy Scutella calling about Charlie. My wife and I were wondering if you would be agreeable to allow us some time with Charlie over Christmas, particularly Christmas day."

"I don't have any problem with that. The boy will be all by himself anyway since I got to waitress that day. I know he sure likes you folks and you treat him really good."

"Thank you so much, ma'am. Actually, my wife and I were wondering if we might be able to meet with you someday to discuss Charlie's situation."

She was hesitant at first, stating she worked most every day and didn't really have any extra time but agreed that, if they were willing to come to the restaurant, she could meet with them a few minutes before her shift started at 3:00. He agreed immediately to see her later that day at the eatery. He then had his front desk cancel his afternoon appointments, so he and Linda could meet with her as soon as possible and before she might change her mind.

The Scutellas arrived at the restaurant at 2:00, both eager to meet with Charlie's grandma. They fidgeted and fretted over cheeseburgers and fries, waiting for her to come in. Andy was a ball of nervous energy and Linda was getting sick to her stomach when a much older, thin woman approximately 4'10" approached their table.

"Are you the Scutellas?" She asked as Andy noticed the irony between the small woman with soft, brown eyes and her loud, scratchy voice.

"Yes", Andy said, jumping up, almost spilling his water across the table. He reached out and grabbed her thin, rough hand, shaking it, "Thank you for meeting with us."

"You're welcome. I'm Esther Wilcox, Charlie's gramma." She slid into the booth across from the Scutellas, pushing the small gray hairs off her face and smoothing them back under her yellow headband. Andy noticed her fingertips were also yellow from many years of cigarette smoke. Her lips etched with lines that her pink lipstick bled into.

Andy explained to Esther that he and Linda were both very fond of Charlie and wondered if she could share with them a little about him and his history. She was pleased to talk about Charlie. It was easy to see she cared a great deal for him. She told them about Charlie's mom, Regina, or Gina, as everyone called her, and her addiction to alcohol and pot that got way out of control after Charlie's dad was killed in a car accident. Charlie was delivered the day his daddy died, and Gina could never seem to get it together. Esther and her husband, Norman, tried to get her help but nothing seemed to work. They loved her so much and desperately tried to help her get back on track. Then Gina met and married Charlie's step-daddy, Dennis. Dennis was an alcoholic too. He was a mean drunk who slapped Gina around and made her work at a bar while he sat on his ass, waiting for her to bring home her paycheck and a six pack or two. Esther told the Scutellas that Charlie had been in the system for years because Gina kept screwing up and getting in trouble. But it got bad when Gina ended up getting pregnant with Dennis's baby. The baby was born with fetal alcohol syndrome and the hospital reported Gina to Child Services who came and took the baby and her rights to the baby away. Gina was supposed to get connected with drug and alcohol treatment to keep Charlie at home, but it wasn't much after the baby was taken that Gina called up the lady who took the baby away and asked her to come take Charlie. The caseworker spoke to Esther and Norman and asked if they would consider fostering Charlie until other arrangements such as a permanent adoption could be made. They both knew how hard it would be to have the young fellow around, especially at their age and with so little money coming in to the household, but they cared for him and couldn't see him placed in a series of strangers' homes. They agreed to keep him there with the goal of finding Charlie a permanent adoptive family. Charlie was dropped off at the Wilcox's house with two plastic shopping bags of belongings and Gina and Dennis skipped town.

It wasn't that long after Charlie went to stay with his grandparents when Norman had a massive heart attack and died. Esther was left to care for Charlie on her own. She explained it had been extremely difficult caring for a growing little boy with the wages of a waitress and working late hours, leaving him all alone to fend for himself. She knew it wasn't what was best for the boy, but she did the best she could

The Scutellas told her how much they loved Charlie and wondered if adoption was an option. They wondered how she felt about the possibility of them providing him with a safe and secure home and adopting him permanently. She cried, tears streamed down the etched paths in her face and landed upon her bright pink lips. She cried because she cared so much for her grandson and the thought of him leaving her killed her inside and she cried because she just had a great weight lifted off her tired shoulders and relief quickly settled in her soul. She told the Scutellas she would like to think about it and talk to Charlie. So, it was agreed that the Scutellas would contact the caseworker and see what options there were and what the process entailed, and Esther would contact them when she was ready.

The next day Esther asked Charlie to come talk to her.

"You know I care about you, don't you boy?"

"Yeah, Gramma," Charlie said, not sure where this was going.

"You know them Scutella folks care about you too."

"They do?" Charlie asked.

"Yeah, boy. They care so much about you they asked me if they could adopt you."

"They did?" He asked setting straight up in his seat, eyes wide open.

"What do you think about them Scutella's?" She asked, watching his face closely.

"I like them a lot. But I don't want to leave you all alone Gramma."

"Boy, you know your old Gramma's getting tired and can't be there for you the way you deserve. You deserve to be a kid and have fun and have good folks who can always be there for you and buy you things and give you things your gramma can't."

"Yeah, Gramma," Charlie said, wanting to stay with the Scutella's but not wanting to hurt his grandmother's feelings.

"I think it's what's best for you, boy. I know you care about me and I'm going to be just fine. I will feel better knowing you are being taken good care of. And we can visit all the time when I'm not at work. What do you think? Would you like that?"

"Yeah, Gramma. I would like that as long as I can keep seeing you."

"Okay, then boy, let's see what we can do. You go ahead now and go to bed while your old gramma finishes her cigarette."

Charlie slid out of his chair and left the tiny kitchen to crawl up into the sofa bed in the next room. He pulled the blanket up to his nose, covering the grin that spread from ear to ear, elated that he may finally have his big family with lots of people to love him.

Esther, on the other hand, slowly dragged on her cigarette, blowing out a puff of smoke that masked the single tear that crept slowly and painfully down her soft, wrinkled cheek and dripped onto her broken heart.

Chapter 34

Kathy was feeling much better since Will's accident and her own small crash and burn. She was beginning to feel the air enter her lungs slowly again after visiting her dad's grave and deciding to give herself permission to practice forgiveness and self-preservation. It was an awakening for her and she started to focus on self-fulfillment. She decided to start doing some of the things she dreamed of doing when she and Chase were sharing future hopes and goals. Why wait? What, exactly, had she been waiting for anyway? She was also getting better at setting personal boundaries, making sure she wasn't assuming any more roles that didn't belong to her. She was keeping work at work, which was easier at the time since a lot of her clients were also experiencing awakenings of their own. She was thrilled the Scutellas were growing closer and stronger, so they could build a strong foundation for Charlie, if all worked out with the adoption as they hoped. Kathy also heard from Janice in the form of a Christmas card that contained a picture of Janice, Emily and Janice's parents standing in front of a gorgeous Florida cottage. Enclosed was a letter from Janice telling Kathy that she and Emily were embraced by her parents when they arrived. She stated they were staying with her parents until she got on her feet. She felt this wouldn't take long as she had already secured a new job as an office manager, thanks to Dr. Scutella's stellar reference. She also went on to say that she signed up for volunteer domestic violence counseling and advocacy training after the new year. She shared that Brad was found guilty of assault and would be in jail for several years. She was choosing to focus on surviving and thriving and learning to love herself again. "It's amazing what negativity you believe when you hear it all the time, repeatedly," Janice said, "Even when it was never true. I hope that Emily learns that no one can take away how special and lovable she is as long as she doesn't give them the power to do so. I'm trying to teach her through my own journey and, every day, I try to love myself a little more. Thank you for helping me to save myself and thank you for reminding me I'm enough. I'm more than enough...I'm worthy and I'm lovable."

Kathy smiled to herself as she placed the letter back into the envelope. She knew exactly how Janice felt. She, too, was falling in love with herself again."

Along with Kathy's attempt to work toward self-acceptance and self-fulfillment, came the creation of a list of things she wanted and needed to do to work toward her goals. She wanted to reduce her sense of doubt, guilt, "shoulds", and personalization. She was going to do her and all of her, good and bad, weak and strong, and she was going to let everybody else do themselves. One day and a time.

There were a variety of things on Kathy's list. It included increasing her social network and supports, trying to find some clothes that didn't look like garbage bags, and getting her hair cut and colored. She had put off getting her hair done for years because she was afraid she wouldn't fit into the salon chairs or would break it if she tried to sit in one. She just got used to settling and cutting her own hair when it needed it.

Kathy also wanted to continue working toward a better relationship with her body. She wanted to be free in all sense of the word and that included within her body. She wanted to dance and swim and run. She wanted to go to places and walk around and fit into booths and movie theater seats. She wanted to breathe deep, glorious, freeing breaths. She wanted to live. She knew she didn't have to be skinny to be loved or attractive or worthy. She was learning to see she was those things simply because she was. Period. She also knew, however, that her body represented a lot of the burden she had been carrying for so long. She wanted to finally remove all the burden. That didn't mean she wasn't going to embrace her curves, roundness, and softness. She always thought full bodies were beautiful. She knew she could find the balance that worked for her, all in good time.

Kathy had been working like an archeologist for a while now. Digging layer by layer to see what she could find, learn, and appreciate about herself. What a marvelous story that was coming to life. There were the layers of pain and shame and guilt and there were the layers of joy and hope and faith. And, she was discovering, they all came together fantastically.

Excited for her outside to communicate the same thing she was feeling inside, Kathy invited her mom to the salon for cuts and colors. Sarah had her shoulder length gray hair cut and colored into a blonde pixie cut and Kathy had her long, red hair shaped and layered with golden highlights surrounding her face. Her curls brushed the top of her shoulders, making her feel both light and pretty.

After the salon, Kathy and Sarah went to lunch. Sarah told Kathy that she visited Will at home. He was complaining about being on crutches but was in better spirits. Will shared what happened the night his car went off the road and how much he thought about his own life. He told her that the ornaments helped him to stay focused and hopeful. He also said they allowed him to remember the good times. He knew he hadn't been easy to be around lately and that he made a lot of mistakes. He realized that in his own hope that everyone would forgive him of his mistakes, he needed to forgive them of theirs.

Sarah told Kathy that Will agreed to let the past go so they could start over again and she was elated to have her son's forgiveness and acceptance once more. Kathy, of course, was delighted to hear they were reunited.

Sarah told Kathy she was going to stay at Will and Amber's house to watch their three golden retrievers. They were going out of town to see a new pain management doctor who has had great success in helping people with the same chronic pain as Will. After the meeting, they had reservations at a hotel for the weekend. They started couples counseling after Will was discharged from the hospital and it was going quite well. Their therapist has been encouraging them to do more one on one activities together to reconnect. So far, so good.

Prior to Will's accident, he and Amber had grown miles apart. Will's anger was contagious. It festered inside until it would erratically break free and ooze over everyone and everything nearby. His negativity was pervasive and his inability to get out of his own misery enough to connect with Amber had played a toll on her and their relationship. She resented him for abandoning her emotionally. She desperately wanted to connect with her husband and only became more withdrawn when he rejected her and pushed her away. Her frustration and disappointment in him then made him feel like she was selfish and didn't care that he was struggling. They were sick, and their love was dying.

It took Will's accident to get him to see what he was losing. The minute he saw her face at the hospital after the accident he swore he would do whatever he could to save his marriage. He would never forget her platinum hair falling over her pale blue, tear filled eyes as she bent down to gently kiss his lips. She squeezed his hand as to never let him go again.

Since they started couples counseling, they have gotten closer. He was working with a counselor individually to address his depression and, with some reduction of his depressive symptoms, he was freed up to start seeing things differently and appreciating what he had in life, which he was finally realizing was abundant, including his beautiful wife.

Sarah explained that they could have had a pet sitter just pop in every now and then over the weekend to care for the dogs, but they were afraid to leave all three out and about with all the Christmas trees and decorations up. "I can't believe they have three Christmas trees up. How did they possibly have enough ornaments to cover all of them?" Kathy asked.

Sarah laughed, "Oh, didn't I tell you Will got all of his ornaments out of the truck before they totaled it?"

"No. How?" Kathy asked.

"Would you believe that nice Officer Phillips boxed up all of Will's stuff out of the truck and took it to the hospital the day he was found? He seems like a very nice man. He's kind of cute too. Don't you think, Kathy? I wonder if he is single."

"Mom," Kathy said, giving her mother a warning look.

Kathy knew she couldn't go there now. Not after Chase and not while she was trying to love and accept herself more. She was happy and getting happier every day. Things were good just where they were...for now.

"Talking about ornaments," Kathy said, "I want to put up my tree tonight if you want to come over and help. You'll be surprised to know I invited Tammy and Mary over for dinner tomorrow night."

"What? You? Being social?" Sarah asked.

"Yeah," Kathy said, "It's part of my new self-acceptance and self-fulfillment plan."

"I love it. That's great. You haven't seen them in a long time, have you?" Sarah asked.

"No. We kept saying we would get together but never did, you know how that goes."

Sarah nodded her head, thinking of her own friends she hadn't seen in a long time. Maybe she should reach out to them too, Sarah thought.

Kathy, Tammy, and Mary all worked together at a community clinic after graduate school. They met there during their internships and were all hired upon completion of their field work and obtaining their degrees.

Tammy left to work for a crime victim service organization and Mary and Kathy both went into private practice. Tammy was a beautiful full-figured woman with dark skin and light brown eyes. She was a married with two boys. Mary was also full figured with porcelain skin and short black, choppy hair. She was single with an eighteen-year-old daughter who was a senior in high school.

Now that the invitations were already accepted and there was no backing out, Kathy found herself having a bit of anticipatory anxiety. What if we have nothing in common anymore? What if I don't know what to say? What if I'm awkward and foolish? What if they think I'm boring? She confronted her own catastrophizing and reminded herself that that type of thinking no longer fit her new goal of self-love and acceptance.

Sarah broke Kathy mirage of "what if's" and stated she would like to help Kathy with the tree so they filled up on lunch and drove to Kathy's where she had already taken the five-foot Spruce out of its dark and dusty slumber and set it up in its stand. It looked so sad and pathetic with it's smooshed, twisted branches reaching out for help.

Kathy giggled to herself thinking she and that tree sure had a lot in common. But before it was all said and done, both would sparkle and shine.

The two ladies wrapped the tree in lights and garland. They went through Kathy's ornaments, including the ones Sarah had gotten her throughout her childhood. The very first one was a small, fuzzy brown mouse wearing a green shirt. There were also a few tiny snow globes, miniature horses and an array of dogs and puppies. All the things Kathy loved the most. A handful of tinsel was placed here and there, and the top of the tree was adorned with a forty-five-year-old, bruised and battered angel in a pink dress with yellow hair, a crooked halo and torn, lacey wings. Kathy and Sarah stood and admired the tree, and both agreed it was, indeed, the most beautiful tree there ever was.

It sat in the front window of Kathy's home, sending a warm glow. It's large colored lights blinking as if it were saying, "There's life in here. There's life in here. There's life in here." The house wasn't feeling as cold and empty as it had. Kathy truly believed it was taking on a new energy, a new life, Kathy's new life. She began to realize her house felt empty and lifeless because that's the way she had felt for so long. She wasn't living in her house, she was existing in it. She wasn't going to just exist anymore. She loved life and it was about time she fully started living it.

Both ladies were exhausted, so they warmed up the ham and bean soup from the freezer, watched a string of silly Christmas romance movies, then went off to bed.

Sarah awoke to the aroma of fresh brewed coffee. She joined Kathy in the kitchen where they both sat at the table with mugs full of equal amounts creamer and coffee. They sliced bananas into warm, gooey oatmeal and chatted about Kathy's dinner party plans.

After Kathy dropped off Sarah, she stopped to buy a bottle of sparkling wine and the groceries she needed. The night's menu consisted of cranberry balsamic roasted chicken with roasted carrots, butternut squash and fingerling potatoes. She had rolls and butter and rich chocolate ganache and berries over angel food cake for dessert.

After rushing home, Kathy prepared the chicken in one pan and the vegetables sprinkled in olive oil and salt and pepper in another. After placing them in the oven, she macerated the berries and put them in the refrigerator to chill. She would prepare the ganache before serving dessert.

She showered, dried her hair, and then got dressed in a teal blue top with black pants and shoes. A swipe of coral lipstick that made her freckles and red hair stand out completed her look. She plugged in the tree and awaited her guests.

Tammy and Mary arrived at the door at the same time. Tammy brought an assortment of cookies she and her children had baked, and Mary brought a bottle of red wine.

Christmas greetings and hugs were shared, and the night was started with glasses of bubbly, sparkling wine. Kathy surprised herself with how comfortable she felt. There was much catching up to do, including careers, family, kids, lovers, and lack thereof. The girls raved about Kathy's cooking. The meal was a delicious combination of sweet and savory. The juicy morsels caramelized and golden.

After dinner, Tammy and Mary cleared the dishes from the table as Kathy prepared the warm, glossy chocolate that she poured over slices of angel food cake, and, then, smothered in sweet berries.

With a few sips of red wine and nibbles of Tammy's cookies, the night was a joyous and spectacular success. The three women agreed

244

to commit to monthly dinners in which they would take turns

hosting. Mary selected next month so schedules were set, hugs were

shared, and Kathy's two guests left for the evening, stepping out and

into the swirling snow.

Chapter 35

Christmas was what Christmas always was. It was a combination

of magic and joy and love, along with heartbreak and loneliness and

stress. It could be a full blown, rapid-cycling bipolar episode of

highs and lows, sometimes, only determined by the luck of the draw.

But Kathy loved Christmas and looked forward to it each year.

This year was especially exciting since she felt her family was

finally safe and reconnected. It had been a difficult and, at times,

nightmarish year but, eventually, the light shone through the

darkness, and many good things had become happily illuminated.

Sarah spent Christmas Eve with Kathy and they spent the evening

preparing food and watching Christmas movies. Sarah made her

deviled eggs and coleslaw and Kathy baked her pumpkin

cheesecake.

Christmas morning was a flurry of action in the kitchen, broken up with bites of fresh, warm sweet rolls and steaming hot, creamy coffee. Kathy glazed her ham in brown sugar and cola. The television was rolling out a marathon of The Christmas Story and Sarah kept Max busy and out of the way.

Kathy was just finishing the preparation of potatoes and candied yams when Will and Amber arrived at the door, bearing gifts. The four Roth family members dove into presents, throwing torn wrapping paper and boxes as they went along. Max was happily involved in the gift wrapping as he tore off pieces of paper from his brand new squeaky ball. It felt so good for Kathy to just let things play out with her family. Initially, she found herself worried that something would happen to set Will off or for Will to reject and ignore Sarah throughout the day. But Kathy reminded herself she wasn't carrying that responsibility anymore. She had to have faith that they would chose to get along and act their age. And they did. They did very well.

Dinner time came, and Will carved the ham, lopping off chunks of sweet and salty, moist morsels of meat and Sarah made her famous ham gravy. Kathy pulled everything together on the dining room table that was decorated with bowls of shiny Christmas bulbs. A chandelier above the table was adorned in garland with the same bulbs hanging down from strings. Candles were lit, and fresh flowers were randomly placed down the center of the table.

Once everyone was seated and Amber said the blessing, she raised her glass and stated, "Here's to Kathy and another delicious holiday meal."

Raising her glass, Kathy responded, "Thank you. Cheers. And here's to family."

In unison, Will and Sarah raised their glasses and added, "To family."

After clinking glasses and diving in, the Roth family Christmas was officially the best Christmas Kathy had seen in a while.

Kathy wasn't the only one who enjoyed her Christmas. Janice and Emily were wrapped in the warm embrace of their family. They were safe and free. Free from fear and violence and free to hope and dream about what the future would have in store for them. Janice had learned through the year that, no matter how bad things seem, there was always hope. If there is absolutely nothing else to hold on to...hold on to hope. Janice and Emily had a joyous holiday season; however, Alicia was always in the forefront of Janice's mind. She lovingly hung Alicia's gifted ornament on her parents' tree and, when it was time to hang up all the family members' individual bulbs with their names on them, Janice and Emily painted one for Alicia and hung it alongside theirs. Janice decided to mourn her friend's death by celebrating her life and making her an honorary family member. She hoped Alicia could look down and see just how loved she was.

Then there were those who struggled during the Christmas day. There was Brad who sat on a hard bed behind bars, staring at a picture of the family he destroyed. He wondered how his little girl, Emily, would remember him. Would she remember when she was younger, and he would play Santa Clause or when he would pick her up to hang the angel on the tree after it was all decorated? Or would she only remember the monster he had become?

There was the shelter full of women and children, trying to survive their own nightmares, trying to hide from their own monsters. They were lost and scared and so damn brave. The mothers pretended everything was going to be just fine and kept the kids entertained as they unwrapped the gifts that Santa remembered to bring them at the shelter because each one of them was so special, he could never forget any of them. All the women joined together in unison and created a multicultural feast, celebrating the holiday, remembering it was Jesus's birthday and praying with everything they had that He would keep them safe and show them the way.

There was a couple of parents, empty and numb, sitting on the very couch they came home to find their dead son, Sam, lying on. His artwork hanging off the walls, serving as constant reminders of their tragic loss. They flatly discussed his first paint set for Christmas and the Labrador puppy he named Cocoa during one special Christmas. They remembered his homemade noodle frames and handprint ashtrays he brought home for them for Christmas. And they remembered his smile. The most beautiful smile in the world, forever lost, never to be seen again. They talked about creating an art therapy program in his name They needed a way to hold onto him, somehow. If they couldn't find a way to hold on, neither one of them was sure they would find a way to carry on.

And then there were the Scutellas. Their home was full of warmth and love like never before. Charlie had come over early Christmas Eve since Esther worked at the restaurant both Christmas Eve and Christmas day.

Charlie ran upstairs to his new bedroom in the Scutellas house and unpacked his backpack. He pulled out two small gifts wrapped in tissue paper and scotch tape.

The week before Christmas, the local fire station took all the kids for Shopping with a Fireman Day. Every year a few of the firemen volunteer to take the kids out to the local supercenter and help them to shop for their families. It was a sponsored community event where each of the children were given twenty dollars to spend.

Charlie had been looking forward to the day because he knew what he wanted to get and who he wanted to buy presents for. When he had finished his shopping, he went home and wrapped his three tiny gifts with tissue paper he found in his grandma's kitchen drawer. A whole roll of tape later, he beamed with pride at what he had just accomplished.

He and Esther traded gifts on Christmas Eve morning. She had knitted Charlie a new hat and glove set out of scratchy black, white and gold colored yarn. They were the colors of his favorite football team. He slid the hat on his head and over his ears. As he did so, he smelled a combination of cigarette smoke, old lipstick, and powder. The combination of scents would conjure up memories for him for the rest of his life. He slid each glove on his hands and said, "Thank you, Gramma. They're awesome."

She, then, pulled out a square box, wrapped in snowman wrapping paper.

"Oh, yeah," she said, "a certain white-haired man in a red suit asked me to give this to you."

Charlie took the box and ripped through the paper to find a clear box filled with old football cards, "Cool!" he screamed, "Thanks Gramma. These are awesome!" he said as he pulled each card out, one by one, reading the stats on the back of the pictures.

Esther had seen the box at a yard sale earlier that year and she talked the woman running the sale to lower the price from fifteen dollars to $6.57. Esther had emptied her wallet out on the table full of knickknacks and costume jewelry, adding every coin. The aging woman, standing in pain, still wearing her restaurant uniform looked devastated to see she didn't have enough. She asked the woman if she could give her what money she had then and bring the rest back the next day, but the woman just smiled and told her to take it. She knew that old box of cards was going to be a very important gift for someone very special.

"Your turn, now, Gramma," Charlie said as he handed her the small wrapped gift, never taking his eyes off his new cards. Esther struggled with the layers of scotch tape until she finally tore the paper away from a small box. She slowly cracked the lid open to see a tiny brassy, gold heart pendant hanging from a similarly brassy chain. She traced the shape of the heart over and over with her index finger.

That brassy old symbol was the closest any of the Wilcox's ever came to mutter the word "love". They just weren't a talkative or demonstrative family. Maybe they should have been.

"'Do you like it Gramma?" Charlie asked, eager to please her.

"Yes, boy. I do like it," she said, looking over at his precious little face, peeking his big eyes out from under his new hat, his hands still inside his new gloves. She smiled to herself and got up out of her chair. She wrapped her arm around his little back and said, "I love it. And I love you, Charlie. Don't ever forget that. Okay?"

"Okay, Gramma."

"You better go get ready. The Scutella's are on their way to pick you up."

"Okay, Gramma."

Not ten minutes later, there was a knock on the door from the Scutellas. Andy stood at the door with a Dutch oven in his hands, still warm and full of roast, potatoes, carrots, and onions. Janet had a loaf of homemade bread in her arms.

"We knew you had to go to work in a little bit, so we wanted to bring you a nice warm lunch."

She thanked them graciously and had Andy place the heavy pot on her stovetop.

"Bye, Gramma," Charlie yelled as he and the Scutella's exited the house.

"Bye, boy. Merry Christmas."

"Merry Christmas," Charlie yelled back as he ran to the car.

Esther slipped her little necklace over her head and sat down to one of the most delicious meals she had in a very long time. She was full of warmth and love that would sustain her over the next two days of having to work at the restaurant. It was amazing how just a small gesture can send a message of love. It was even more amazing to express the feeling of love. She would never let that little boy go without knowing she loved him. She, now, knew the importance of openly sharing her love and letting those she loved to know it.

When the Scutellas and Charlie got home they, too, sat down to warm, delicious roast and vegetables. But everybody was so full of joy and excitement they needed to burn off some energy. They layered up and piled back in the car and went sledding. After sledding, they spent a couple of hours driving around looking at

Christmas lights while they sang and laughed. They were all simply elated to be in each other's company.

They eventually found their way back home. After about half an hour of a Christmas movie, Charlie was passed out on the couch, snoring. Andy gently woke Charlie and told him to go up to bed and then the couple sat together, nuzzling and cuddling on the couch. After the movie, they pulled the Christmas presents out of the closet and placed them under the Christmas tree. They already had a few under there for each other.

They weren't exactly sure what to do for Charlie's Christmas They didn't want to go overboard but also wanted him to have a nice day. They agreed on a little fun and a little practical. After everything was arranged under the tree, they stood back and looked at their tree sparkling and lit up, shiny packages and bows underneath for a child they never thought they would have. With a kiss on the lips and a smack from Andy on Linda's butt, they headed upstairs to crash.

Andy and Linda awoke Christmas morning and crept down the stairs, trying not to wake up Charlie. But when they got to the landing, they seen Charlie asleep, under the tree, and with two little tissue paper wrapped gifts in his hand. They tiptoed through the living room into the kitchen where Janet started the coffee and Andy pulled out a breakfast casserole he had already cooked. He placed it in the oven to get warm and then turned around to see Charlie coming into the kitchen.

"Well, good morning sleepy head. Did you happen to notice there were a few things left for you under the tree?" Andy asked. "You better go see what's under there." Charlie was off running.

They all sat on the floor, circling the tree. Charlie said, "Wait! These are from me." Then he handed each of them their gift he brought for them. He was grinning from ear to ear.

"Wow. Really? For us?" Andy asked.

"That was so sweet," Linda said.

"Open them," he said excitedly.

They both tore through the paper and tape like little children. Linda pulled out a key chain with a picture of Wonder Woman on it.

She laughed out loud, "It's perfect, Charlie. I love it. Thank you so much." She reached beside her and wrapped her arm around his back. He was so happy. He knew he nailed it.

Andy pulled out a key chain too but his was a movable figuring that looked like a Superman with dark hair and a cape but the words across the chest of the figurine were like nothing he thought he would ever see. He cupped the figuring in his hand, wiped away a tear from his eye, and read the words out loud, "You're my hero." He reached over to Charlie and pulled him over to him. He embraced him, and held him close to his chest. Charlie had never been hugged like that before. He let out a long, heavy sign and softened into Andy's chest and just soaked it up. Andy kissed the top of Charlie's head and said, "I love my present and I love you, Charlie. Thank you so much. Now come on, let's start ripping these babies open." A whirlwind of paper and boxes and bows were flung around the living room until each person had a small pile of treasures. Linda had a new charm bracelet. Andy had a new leather coat. And Charlie had a few new comic books, a video game, a sled, a pack of socks, and a new pair of winter boots from his soon to be adoptive parents.

Afterwards, the three of them had a little breakfast casserole and then Andy started attacking the kitchen. There was a Christmas feast to prepare. Both Andy's dad and Linda's parents came to dinner, along with Kyle, Beth, and Kaleb.

They all gathered around the table. No blessing was given in the Scutella home as they were non-believers, but something was happening inside of Andy. Something was stirring in his soul. His deepest wishes had been coming true and no one really knew about those wishes. Of course, he and Linda had tried to have a baby and then gave up when everything started to spiral downward for them. And he had spoken to Kathy in his counseling sessions about wanting a child, a family. But the real thing he ever put out into the universe was a desperate plea, one day when he felt so empty and meaningless, he looked to the sky and he said, "If there is a God somewhere up there, please save me from this loveless, meaningless life. Please show me the answers I need to find happiness and fulfillment." That was it. Nothing happened right away, and he forgot about the plea and eventually just got more and more disillusioned. Perhaps there was something to timing. Perhaps, there were plans he knew nothing about. Perhaps there was a God, after all.

Everything was delicious. Once again, there was laughter and talking and clinking of china and chattering of ice. And, once again, Charlie found himself thinking the same thing he did at Thanksgiving, "So this is what a big, happy family looks and sounds like." Except this time, he said, "My family."

Everything was coming together for the three of them. Would they be able to keep it together?

Chapter 36

Christmas morning and afternoon went by like a whirlwind and it became time for Charlie to go back home to Esther's house. She would be home from work by the time he arrived. Charlie gathered the gifts he received and decided what he want to take back to his grandmother's and what he wanted to keep at the Scutella's.

Andy prepared a dinner plate and collected the caramel apple pie he made for Esther and then they all piled in the car. When they arrived at Esther's house there was a small, green Ford parked in the drive. A lovely woman in her early thirties was pulling a large suitcase out of the trunk. She had sandy hair like Charlie's and full red lips. She was small in stature like Charlie as well. Charlie was so busy playing his new video game that he didn't even notice the woman at first.

"Charlie, Linda said, "It looks like you and your gramma have company."

Charlie looked up and peered out the window. His eyes grew as big as saucers and he yelled, "Mom!"

Charlie threw open the door and raced out of the car as he ran to the woman, "Mom!" Andy's heart began to race, and he and Linda looked at each other in panic. They both jumped out of the car and hurried after Charlie.

The small, lip stained woman wrapped her arms around Charlie and clung to him, holding him tight against her chest. The two of them hugged and rocked in each other's arms for what seemed liked hours to the two panicked onlookers.

"Mom, what are you doing here?" Charlie asked her not letting go of his mom who, not long ago, rejected and abandoned him.

She pulled away from the love-struck fellow, stumbling backwards a bit, and said, "I'm here to take you back, Charlie." The smile on Charlie's face instantly fell. He recognized the smell of alcohol on her breath and the way he said his name, long and drawn out

All the hope filled air was sucked dry, leaving the Scutellas gasping. Andy jumped to catch the woman when she stumbled, dropping his keys in the snow. He watched the Superman figurine that Charlie just gave him for Christmas sinking deep into the snow and hurried to collect it, feeling around desperately for his symbol of hope and meaning with one hand and extending another out to the woman who, when observed closer, looked sedated and worn.

"I'm Charlie's momma, Regina. You must be the folks trying to take my baby away from me."

We love your son very much," Linda said, feeling the sharpness of the woman's words cut through her chest. "There must be a misunderstanding. Is Esther here?" She asked, holding the Christmas offerings close to her and in between herself and this woman who threatened her happiness.

Just then, the door opened, and Esther exited, "I see you got a chance to meet Regina, who paid an unexpected visit."

"I came to get my damn kid and then I'm out of here."

"You're not even supposed to be here, Regina. You're going to get yourself in a mountain of trouble. Look at you. You're drunk. You don't have any right to that boy, Gina. Leave him alone. Give him a chance to have something good in his life."

"You want to come live with your momma, don't you, Charlie. I'm doing good now. I don't drink like I used to no more. I've changed now, Charlie."

"I don't know," Charlie said, backing away from his mother.

"Ah, Jesus, Gina! Leave the boy alone."

"Come on, boy. Give your momma a kiss," Regina stepped closer to Charlie, arms wide open. He turned and ran to Andy and Linda, scared and confused.

"Get back here, boy. Don't you dare treat your momma like that."

Andy, with his arm around Charlie, slid him around behind his leg and interrupted, saying, "You know it's been a long day and you've been traveling all day. Everyone is tired. Why don't we take Charlie back to our house and then we will come by tomorrow to discuss this issue?"

"That sounds like a good idea," Esther said, "You take Charlie back home with you and we can get some rest and talk in the morning." She reached out and grabbed the treats Linda held close to her chest, "Thank you both. You're really good folks."

"Good folks? Good folks wouldn't be trying to take my kid. You're not taking my boy anywhere," Gina said.

"Come on, Charlie," Andy and Linda surrounded the boy and walked him back to the car and locked the doors.

Gina ran toward the car, "You can't take my kid," she said, pounding on the hood of the car. She circled around to Charlie's window and knocked on the glass, "Charlie! Charlie! Don't leave your momma. Don't leave me, Charlie! I need you!"

Charlie sobbed in the back of the car, terrified and confused. Regina dropped on her knees in the snow, crying, "Charlie, don't do this to me. Why are you doing this to me?"

The car pulled away, leaving the heartbroken woman sobbing in the snow. Charlie turned to see his mother lying there in a fetal position, all the neighbors out of their toasty, dreamy Christmas-filled homes, watching his worst nightmare.

The Scutellas vehicle turned the corner as the police and ambulance that Esther called arrive in front of the house. They loaded Gina into the ambulance and transported her to the hospital where she would be admitted into mental health for the fourth time in her life.

The next day, Esther tried to visit with Gina, but she just laid in her bed hugging her knees to her chest and staring at the wall. "Just go home, Momma," Gina said and turned her back on her. Esther tried to tell her about the meeting she and the Scutellas had with the caseworker that morning, but Gina said nothing. Esther told Gina that the caseworker provided approval for the Scutellas to start the adoption process. Esther thought Gina should know this, so she could process all of this with her counselors. Gina continued to lie away from her, saying nothing. After a few moments, Esther reached out and touched Regina's arm.

"Gina?", she asked, desperate to connect with her.

"I said go away," Gina yelled through gritted teeth.

Esther picked up her pocketbook off the chair by Gina's bed, whispered the words "I love you", and walked out without another word.

Esther waited a couple of days, mainly because she had to work long hours at the restaurant, and then she went back to the hospital to visit Gina. Hopefully she was feeling better and opening to the staff so that she could get the help she needed. Maybe this time would work, and Esther would finally have her daughter back.

Esther pushed the button beside the door and announced herself to be buzzed in. She was greeted by the caseworker she met the last time she tried to visit with Gina. The caseworker stated that Gina had left the program AMA that morning. She told Esther, "A man by the name of Dennis picked her up this morning. She wasn't a safety risk to herself, so we couldn't make her stay here. The doctors advised her that it would be best for her to stay and work toward recovery, but she declined our services. She did ask me to give this to you if you came by," she handed a folded-up piece of paper with the words Momma and Charlie scrawled across the front.

Esther, sad and angry to hear Regina left treatment again and didn't even bother to say goodbye, took the letter and cupped it with both hands against her chest.

"Sorry," the caseworker whispered as she reached out and rested her hand on Esther's back.

Esther forced a smile and thanked her. She opened the piece of paper and read the contents of the letter as she walked slowly toward the exit door. By the time she made it to the big door separating the mental health unit from the rest of the hospital, she finished reading the letter, ripped it into several pieces, and dropped it in a nearby wastebasket.

She pushed her way through the heavy door and back into reality where a few penned out lies, promises, and "somedays" didn't make everything all better. Esther didn't have "someday". Her "somedays" were almost gone. And the only thing anyone ever really has for sure is "now".

Esther didn't believe in sugar coating things. When she returned home from the hospital, she told Charlie his mother discharged, and she and Dennis left the state again.

Charlie nodded his little head and said, "She's sick, Gramma. You did the best you could." Esther chuckled, patted his head and said, "I suppose I did, boy. I suppose I did."

Chapter 37

Christmas came and went and gave way to New Year's Eve. Will and Amber planned the first New Year's Eve party that they have had for many years. They were doing well together, and Will was feeling good and enjoying life again. They decided it could be a good opportunity to celebrate the new year and thank all the folks that helped during Will's accident, including family, friends, a couple officers, Jeff Bailey, the ER doctor and some of the other hospital staff.

Amber made the best strawberry daiquiris and they also provided beer and champagne. They had tables covered with delectable foods including fruit, dips, salads, deli trays and rolls, and a cake with the words, "Here's to new beginnings".

The house was festive with sparkling, bright lights trimming the outside facade and the interior doors and windows. All three of the Christmas trees were lit up throughout the house and were being admired by the many guests that had already arrived.

Officer Tommy Phillips attended the party with his coworker, Officer Nicholas Daniels. Nicholas already abandoned Tommy for a brunette and Tommy was left waiting. Waiting and hoping that the woman he had his eye on would show up. It was getting late and he was beginning to doubt she would come.

Kathy was running around her house, trying to get ready for Will and Amber's party. She was feeling great about the new year and what was in store for her and all the people in her life. She felt she finally made amends with a lot of her past and chose to incorporate all her experiences into her story. She was no longer trying to pound a circle into a square and decided to embrace herself, right where she was, who she was, and where she came from. It was all a part of her and she was at peace. She felt like nothing could hold her back anymore and the party was just what she needed to celebrate her accomplishments.

Although, she was a large woman, she appreciated her image in the mirror. After showering and drying her hair, she slid a new top on that she purchased for the occasion. It was emerald green with sapphire blue gems around the collar. Her long, red hair rested upon her shoulders and the gems peaked out from under her curls. She swept a light green powder on her eye lids which gave her warm brown eyes a soft glow. She brushed a sparkling pink-coral blush on her cheeks and a gorgeous coral gloss on her full lips. A final touch with emerald earrings and a black cape coat and she was ready to go. One New Year's Eve biscuit for Max and she was on her way to celebrate.

By time she got to Will and Amber's house, there were quite a few folks streaming in and out of the party. She couldn't help but notice Will's two co-workers Grace and Dora were coming up behind her, looking stunning as ever. "Hi, girls," she said, thinking she would like to catch them on fire. They waved and acknowledged her as well. Just as Kathy reached the door, it opened, and she was face to face with Officer Tommy Phillips.

"Oh, hi, Officer Phillips. How are you? Are you leaving?"

Tommy, who had just decided to leave, determining the woman

he was hoping to see wasn't coming, responded, "Hi, Kathy. Yes, I was thinking about it."

She noticed him looking over her head and realized he was staring at Grace and Dora. "Oh, Tommy, these are Will's co-workers, Grace and Dora."

"Yes," he said, "we met when I dropped off Will's truck contents at the hospital."

"Hi, girls," he said, his sparkling eyes smiling at them.

Kathy slipped into the door after realizing she was in the way, and left Officer Phillips with the two giggling girls. For whatever reason, she found herself hurting a little that he gave them his attention. But she reminded herself this was a day to celebrate and found her way to Will, Amber, and Sarah.

Kathy had a blast. Everyone was enjoying themselves taking in good food, good drink, and great company.

Curiosity got the best of Kathy and she glanced around the room a couple of times to see if Officer Phillips decided to stay. She spotted him across the room, talking to Grace. Kathy met his eyes once and he smiled at her from a distance. Her heart pounded a little and her stomach did a little flip-flop. What the hell was happening there? She wasn't even wanting to go there right now. But, damn it! His eyes were such a unique colored blue, when she looked into them, it was like bathing in a warm pool of water with the sun piercing the surface, lighting up the depths below. She just wanted to dive in. And the blue button up shirt he wore, with the buttons pulling at his tummy was too much. She shook her head and went over to join Sarah.

The next time Kathy looked for Officer Phillips, he was no longer talking to Grace. He was talking to Will and Amber. Then Amber started to yell, "Here we go everyone....10, 9, 8..."

Tommy began to panic, he couldn't let the night end without stealing a kiss from that amazing woman. But, what if she isn't interested?"

"7, 6, 5..."

Kathy turned to see everyone starting to join together, holding each other in their arms, sharing romantic smiles, and then she seen

Officer Phillips. He looked like he was looking for someone too. She

circled around, looking for Grace, but she was in the arms of

another. She looked back up at Tommy and he was coming straight

at her.

"4, 3, 2..."

He slipped an arm around Kathy's waist and pulled her into him,

"May I?", he asked, looking into her eyes.

"1"

She nodded, and he pressed his lips softly on hers', squeezing her

tight into him. She reached up to place her hand on his back, holding

him close.

He slowly pulled away, smiling at her with those eyes, he said,

"Happy New Years, Kathy."

"Happy New Years, Officer Phillips," she said as he began to

walk away.

"Tommy", he said, looking back at her, still smiling, beaming, actually.

"Tommy," she replied as a bright crimson red colored her cheeks.

He smiled to himself. He just kissed the woman he had waited for all night. She was the woman he wanted. But he knew, if she was to ever be his, he had to respect her space and her independence and give her the time she needed to consider being with him. He knew that she would be his when she was ready.

Chapter 38

Esther had two whole days off in a row, which was rare for her. Since she worked all of Christmas Eve and Christmas Day, she got New Year's Eve and New Year's Day off. It was perfect timing. She and Charlie started going through the house and tried to organize piles of items to throw away, to give to the thrift and to take with them. They were, both, about to start new adventures.

The Scutellas were attending a New Year's Eve staff party on

New Year's Eve night so Charlie stayed home with his grandma. It was a big night for them and she agreed to let Charlie stay up to watch the giant ball in New York City drop at midnight on the television.

Esther and Charlie drove down to the Dollar Store and bought spray cheese and crackers and a bottle of sparkling grape juice. Charlie was thrilled that he was going to be able to stay up to midnight. Esther made eggs and toast for their dinner and then they worked a bit on the house. About 8:00 that night, they finished their housework, turned on the television and enjoyed their cheese and crackers and grape juice in fancy champagne glasses. Charlie tried and tried to stay awake but eventually fell asleep around 10:30. Esther followed shortly after him. She didn't need to celebrate the event, she knew great things were in store for Charlie and herself.

Charlie was getting close to moving in with the Scutellas and Esther was getting close to being able to sell the old, run down house and move into a residential facility with her own apartment and plenty of staff to take care of any problems. She was looking forward to getting out from under that house and all the burden it placed on her shoulders. She had been oppressed by that house and the memories buried in it for too long. There were stories in that house that no one spoke of and Esther was getting so tired of carrying the weight. Her ravenous craving for freedom ate at her spine where fear and heartbreak co-habituated. She still wasn't sure which would ultimately prevail.

Esther knew she had to leave the house and move forward. She was seventy-two years old and didn't have the physical energy or the finances to maintain the house anymore. She was hoping to be able to reduce some of her hours, especially knowing Charlie would be well cared for. She knew he would never want or need anything now that the Scutellas were going to be his foster parents. She thanked God for bringing the Scutellas into their lives because they were saving them both.

As the Scutellas were taking on Charlie and his care more and more, they found themselves equally enjoying time with Esther. Andy found himself feeling like she was the mother he was missing in his life.

Linda was going over to Esther's a lot when Andy was at work. That way she could spend more time with Charlie and help Esther go through over fifty years of "stuff" that accumulated in her tiny 786 square foot ranch home. The house had a kitchen, a living room, two bedrooms, and a tiny bathroom that housed a shower only, providing enough room for the water heater and a stackable washer and dryer. One of the bedrooms was filled with layers of things that were shoved in there when there was no more room in the rest of the house. That's why Charlie slept on the sofa bed in the living room. There was no way Esther would be able to go through that room on her own, or any of the rooms, for that matter.

Linda noticed one day when she was packing up pictures from the walls and shelves in the living room that there were no pictures of Gina. As a matter of fact, there were only pictures of Charlie, Norman, and Esther, herself. Her curiosity began to grow as she continued to go through the house. Something just wasn't adding up.

Andy would stop by Esther's after work to see Charlie and help Linda and Esther do any moving or heavy lifting that accrued throughout the day. He liked Esther and felt closer to her each day.

He appreciated her straightforwardness and her tough approach to life. She was kind and warm, but she told you how it was, and she stepped up to the plate when she needed to. He knew she had been stepping up for a long time now and her soft, warm eyes showed weariness. She was a survivor. He had a feeling life had been harder on her than anyone really knew, and he hoped someday he might learn a lot more about her and from her.

Between the four of them, they were slowly getting through the accumulated years that filled Esther's house. The Scutella's took several loads of stuff to the thrift store. They took the boxes of things Esther wanted to use in her new apartment and placed them in her bedroom and then loaded the curbside with several bags of garbage.

The only big project left was the second bedroom, stuffed wall to wall and layer by layer, ready to burst.

"I'll be over next week, Esther, and we can start on your spare room," Linda called to Esther one night as she was getting ready to go for the evening.

"Oh, no, Linda. That's okay. I think I will work on that room by myself, " Esther said without hesitation.

"Are you sure, Esther? There's so much in there and I can help," Linda stated, trying to convince her she didn't need to do it alone.

"No. I'm sorry but I don't want your help with that room."

Confused by Esther's reaction, Linda simply retreated. Andy put his arm around Linda to acknowledge Esther's behavior toward Linda was odd. "Well, we're off for now," he said, "Let us know if you need anything. Bye Charlie. See you tomorrow."

"Bye," Charlie yelled back as they were exiting the house.

"Thank you for everything Linda and Andy. You've been so helpful, and I appreciate everything you've done", Esther told them as they smiled and left for the night.

"What the hell was that?" Andy asked when they got to the car.

"I don't know," Linda responded, "It feels like there's something she doesn't want us to know about or something she is avoiding."

"I agree. I think there's more to Esther than meets the eye," Andy said as he started humming the Twilight Zone theme music.

Linda laughed and slapped his arm, "Stop that! You're freaking me out."

She told Andy about her noticing there were no pictures of Gina in the house.

"Hmm. That is weird, isn't it? There's a mystery here, isn't there? You want to make a bet who's the first one to figure out what is going on?"

"You're on," Linda said.

Chapter 39

Charlie found himself wondering what was in that spare room too. His grandma wasn't letting him help either. He had been living there for quite some time and was never allowed in the room.

When Charlie spent time at the Scutella's, Esther would work on the room. He knew that because when the Scutella's dropped him off, Esther would have more items for them to haul to the curb or to take to the thrift store. She was often fatigued, flat, and left with red, swollen eyes, making Charlie and the Scutella's worry about her ability to get through the entire room.

One weekday, when Charlie was back at school after the holiday and Esther was at work, she became ill. She felt so sick and unsteady on her feet that she called Linda and asked her to come pick her up at work and take her home. Linda was pleased to do so. It just so happened that Andy was home too since he took a vacation day for the couple to share a long weekend end together. The two hurried to the restaurant to pick up Esther. Andy took the family car and Linda followed him in Esther's car back to her house.

He examined her a bit and felt she was overdoing things and needed to slow down and take better care of herself.

Linda made Esther some tea and Andy warmed up some soup from the cupboard. She began to feel a little better and a little more energized. After eating her soup, she began to go through her phone messages from the old answering machine setting on the kitchen table.

"Hello, Mrs. Wilcox. This is Mr. Roddick from the elementary school calling to check on Charlie since he didn't attend school today. You can call me at 827-2715. Thank you," was a message left sometime earlier in the day.

"What? Where's Charlie?" Andy asked, didn't he go to school today?"

Esther said, "He was getting ready for school when I left for work today. He was going to take the bus like he usually does. He's never not gone to school before," Ester said in panic.

"Charlie?' Andy called as he went outside to look for him.

"Charlie?" Linda started looking around the house.

Worried, and not really thinking, Esther ran over to the spare bedroom, swung open the door, and gasped, "Charlie!"

Andy and Linda both ran to the open door of the spare room and, there on the bed decorated with sports figures all over the blanket and pillows, was little Charlie curled up, asleep. He was peacefully encapsulated in time. There were posters of sports figures all over the wall. Baseball bats sat in the corner of the room. A basketball hoop hung on the back of the door. The dresser was lined in various sports related trophies and a framed picture of Esther, Norman, and a young boy that looked much like Charlie with his big brown eyes and long eye lashes. The same sandy hair fell over the boy's eyes, just like Charlie's hair fell over his eyes. There was a framed picture of that same boy, standing, in uniform, with a team of baseball players.

The Scutellas were in awe as they tried to make sense of what they were seeing. Everything in that room screamed, "A boy lived here." Who was the boy? What about Gina?

Esther sighed and sat on the bed beside Charlie who was already awake. He jumped out of the bed and tried to fix the blanket to make it look the way he found it, "I'm sorry, Gramma. Please don't be mad."

"It's okay, Charlie. Come. Sit with your old Gramma. I have some explaining to do."

"The room that you all are in belonged to your daddy, Charlie. My son, Johnathan. When your mom, Gina, went into labor with you, she and Johnathan were at Gina's parents' house having dinner." She lowered her head and began to cry.

"It was snowing really hard that day and the roads were covered in ice. Everyone piled into the car to get Gina to the hospital and Johnathan was driving. He lost control of the car when he took the exit to the hospital. The car flipped off the ramp and then a couple more times. Gina was the only one who survived, and she gave birth to you in the ambulance. You were truly a little miracle, Charlie."

Looking up at the Scutellas, Esther explained, "Norman and I were so devastated that Johnathan died that we submerged ourselves into being there for Gina and Charlie. We tried to take Gina under our wing since her parents were killed but she spiraled downward and got into the drugs and, eventually, met Dennis. One bad thing led to another."

Esther looked at Andy and Linda, "Gina is my daughter-in-law, not my daughter. My baby boy was taken on that day. I never really mourned him. I took all reminders of him and sealed his memory in this bedroom. Norman and I never talked about him. We never talked about our loss. We never talked to Gina about what happened. I often wonder if things would have worked out differently with her if we had. We just never were the talking kind. We just did what we had to do to move on. So, over the years, I just kept shoving more layers of stuff into his room, just like I did inside myself."

"I see your daddy in you every day, boy," Esther said as she reached out to Charlie, pulling him closer, "He was sweet and hard-working, and he had your beautiful eyes. He would have been so proud of you, Charlie. He told me a week before he died that he would lay his head on your momma's belly and listen to your heartbeat. He told me, no matter what he did in life, he would make sure you knew you were loved."

Charlie smiled at Esther, "Thank you, Gramma. I'm sorry you're sad."

"Sadness is part of life, boy, but it's not the only part," Esther said, "There is good and bad, happy and sad, but most of all, no matter how long you have it, it's a gift."

"Wait a minute," Andy said, all of sudden looking confused and in awe, "Johnathan Wilcox? When I was doing my internship at Community Hospital, I was one of the doctors working on a young man named Johnathan Wilcox who was in an accident with his pregnant wife. When was the accident?" he asked.

"In January. The car slid on the ice in January," Esther recalled.

"And he knew he was having a baby boy?" Andy asked.

"Yes. He was so proud to be having a boy. Why?" Esther asked.

Andy reached into his back pocket and opened his wallet. "Right before we lost him, Johnathan, gave me something that he was holding in his hand the whole time we were working on him. All he said was, 'Make sure he knows I love him.' I tried to get it to his wife. I wrote her a couple of letters. I tried a few times to call her. She never responded to any of my outreach and I, eventually, gave up trying. I could never throw it away, though. Each time I changed my wallet, I carried it over to the new one. I never knew why. I just couldn't get rid of it."

Esther said, "We moved Gina right in with us after the accident. She never went back to their apartment again. She said it was too hard to go back there. Then she got into the drugs and the abusive men and the nervous breakdowns and that's probably why you were never able to find her."

"Well, so what is it? What did he give you?" Everyone wanted to know.

Andy pulled the worn and tattered paper out of a pocket in his wallet and handed it to Esther and Charlie. It was a black and white sonogram picture with the words "Baby Boy Wilcox, Due Date January 2009".

Chapter 40

Everything was going well in the new year. Kathy continued to feel good about herself, her body, and the work she was doing with her clients.

Tommy called Kathy and asked her out about two weeks after the New Year's Eve kiss. She'd spent those two weeks in a sense of dreamy apprehension, having gotten blown away by his amazing kiss and wondering what it would be like to kiss him again, yet, not wanting to get into another mess like with Chase. But Tommy felt different to her. Her warning bells weren't going off like they did with Chase. She felt safe and protected around him. She felt beautiful in his eyes. There was no leaping, though. They both agreed to take it one day at a time.

Kathy's family was doing well. Her mother was enjoying her life and spending time with her family, free of guilt and shame. She was rebuilding her relationship with Will and finding enjoyable pursuits.

Will and Amber were closer than ever. They made efforts to spend alone time together and engage with one another. They shared their days and their concerns. They supported each other. And, most importantly, they reminded each other every day how much they loved and needed each other. The strong, loving family Kathy needed and wanted had come to fruition and the group of them made efforts to spend more time together for weekly dinners or game nights.

Many of Kathy's clients were moving on from therapy, having achieved their treatment and personal goals. For all the ones that were moving on, there were new ones starting with their own set of treatment and personal goals.

The Scutellas were growing into a beautiful family with Charlie and Esther and the adoption process was going well.

Andy and Linda attended a session with Kathy and told her all about Charlie's dad and the picture Andy had carried for so long. She was fascinated by the story and was curious how they chose to talk to themselves about everything that had occurred. They both agreed that they were beginning to believe that there was a higher power and that, maybe there were divine plans in place. At the very least. they were both able to believe that their story was a miraculous one. They were humbled to be the stars of such a glorious story of renewal and love. They thanked Kathy for helping them through their long journey and they all agreed they were ready to terminate their counseling sessions and move on.

Kathy got a letter from Janice, stating she and Emily continued to do well. Emily was excelling in school and Janice, not only loved her job, but officially completed her volunteer training and was working as a Domestic Violence Counselor and Advocate.

Sam accomplished in death what he could only dream of when he was alive. It turned out he already had several people who believed in him and appreciated him more than he would have ever believed. When they heard his parents were trying to create a program in his name, they were pleased to donate and sponsor the program. His parents collected enough donations to fund the Samuel Steinman Art Therapy Program which was approved for development. His purpose and meaning would grow through the folks that would participate in recovery through his program. He couldn't save himself, but he would be able to help save others. Perhaps that was the way it was meant to be. Kathy once heard that the giant Oak must die to give life to the saplings below. Perhaps that was true about Sam. One thing she knew for sure, Sam was brought into her life, not the other way around. It was her connection with Sam and her desperate need to save him that helped her to find peace with not being able to save her father. Sam taught her that she couldn't control or save others, she could just love, support, and accept them. He allowed her to see past her resentment toward George, the absent father, to George, the man who suffered through his own battles. Sam allowed her to see her father deserved forgiveness and love too. He tried, they both did; unfortunately, addiction puts up one hell of fight and, all too often, wins.

Chapter 41

After a particularly busy day full of new clients, Kathy marveled at how the human spirit continued to fight and carry on. She thought about how many folks walked through her door, ready to give up, not believing they could fight a minute longer, not believing they were worthy of the fight and, with the tiniest fraction of faith that got them to her door and the human spirit that naturally wants to survive and thrive, they could make it through to the other side. She marveled at how special each person was that came into her office. Most of them wanting to be loved, accepted, and appreciated. Most of them, afraid of being judged and determined as less than everybody else, not good enough, and not worthy. Most of them having completely distorted the images they created of themselves. They were each unique and gifted. The mere fact that they existed made them worthy enough and good enough. The secret trick was for them to stop trying to become someone altogether different and, instead, accept their own gifts, their own strengths, their own vulnerabilities, and their own weaknesses. They needed to learn how to use their strengths, their powers for good, and how to work around their weaknesses, and, yes, at times, modify their weaknesses. And if they could truly embrace the whole package that they were, how God made them and how they were put on this earth, they would see and understand that there was absolutely no way they could ever really be unlovable.

Made in the USA
Middletown, DE
14 July 2018